'W [illegible] he sai[illegible] ed towards her, as relaxed and as determined as a tiger moving in on its cornered prey.

'[illegible], I know, but I'm [illegible] own n[illegible]. For you[illegible] tered w[illegible] intent a[illegible] her s[illegible]nach. She [illegible] of p[illegible]sion in his [illegible] flame, s[illegible]ook a coup[illegible] wards him, reaching o[illegible] and then sti[illegible] a moan of response as he p[illegible]led her towards him.

A[illegible]dreas felt a powerful surge of possession as hi[illegible] mouth descended on hers. She had offered ha[illegible]f-hearted protests, and it was to her credit that sh[illegible] hadn't leapt upon his generous suggestion th[illegible]t she accompany him back to London when th[illegible] time came for him to take his leave, but her ac[illegible]quiescence now felt good.

H[illegible] continued to kiss her as he propelled her t[illegible] short distance to his desk, at which point he e[illegible]ortlessly lifted her so that she was sitting on the desk in front of him.

'[illegible] of my fantasies,' he said hoarsely, as he unb[illegible]ttoned her white shirt with unsteady fingers. 'M[illegible] desk in London is as big as a bed, but I've never wondered what it would be like to see my woman splayed out naked on it.'

Cathy Williams is originally from Trinidad, but has lived in England for a number of years. She currently has a house in Warwickshire, which she shares with her husband Richard, her three daughters, Charlotte, Olivia and Emma, and their pet cat Salem. She adores writing romantic fiction, and would love one of her girls to become a writer—although at the moment she is happy enough if they do their homework and agree not to bicker with one another!

POWERFUL BOSS, PRIM MISS JONES

BY

CATHY WILLIAMS

First published in Great Britain 2010
Harlequin Mills & Boon Limited,
Eton House, 18-24 Paradise Road, Richmond, Surrey TW9 1SR

ISBN: 978 0 263 87797 7

Harlequin Mills & Boon policy is to use papers that are natural, renewable and recyclable products and made from wood grown in sustainable forests. The logging and manufacturing process conform to the legal environmental regulations of the country of origin.

Printed and bound in Spain
by Litografia Rosés, S.A., Barcelona

POWERFUL BOSS, PRIM MISS JONES

CHAPTER ONE

'NO, NO and no. I couldn't have that woman around me. Did you notice that she had a moustache?' James Greystone, seventy-two years old, and at present sedately ensconced in his wheelchair by the bay window which overlooked some of the sprawling acreage that encompassed his estate, did nothing to conceal his horror at the thought of it. At the mere suggestion of it. 'The woman would be better suited to boot camp. She had a voice like a foghorn and the body of a sumo wrestler. I'm shocked that you would even *entertain* the thought of having her anywhere near me!' Having dismissed this latest casualty, he settled his gaze on his godson, who was leaning against the wall, hands casually in his trouser pockets, feet lightly crossed at the ankle.

Andreas sighed and strolled to join his godfather at the bay window where he looked out in silence at lawns leading down to fields, culminating in a copse which was barely visible in the distance. The late-summer sunshine gave the gently rolling, peaceful landscape a picture-postcard beauty.

He never forgot that all this—the grounds, the magnificent house, every single appendage of a lifestyle his father could never in a million years have afforded—was his thanks to the old man sitting in the wheelchair next to him. James

Greystone had employed Andreas's father as his chauffeur and general odd-job man at a time when finding employment for an immigrant had not been easy. He had accommodated Andreas's mother when, two years later, she had appeared on the scene and had similarly found suitable work for her to do. In the absence of any of his own children, when Andreas had arrived he had treated him as his own. Had put him through the finest schools, schools that had helped to develop Andreas's precocious and prodigious talents. Even now Andreas could remember his father sitting in the same room as they were in now, playing the old man at a game of chess with his cup of coffee going cold on the table next to him.

Andreas owed James Greystone pretty much everything, but there was far more to their relationship than duty. Andreas loved his godfather even though he could be grumpy, eccentric and—as he was now—virtually impossible.

'She's the twenty-second person we've interviewed, James.'

His godfather grunted and maintained a steady silence as Maria, his faithful retainer of well over fifteen years now, brought him the small glass of port which he knew he was technically not really allowed to drink.

'I know. It's impossible to get good staff these days.'

Andreas did his best not to indulge his godfather's sense of humour. With very little encouragement James Greystone would derail the whole interviewing process, because he just didn't like the fact that he needed a carer, someone to help him with his exercises, handle some of his paperwork and take him out of the house now and again. He didn't like the wheelchair which he was temporarily obliged to use. He didn't like having to ask anyone to lend him a hand doing anything. He didn't want anyone to have the final say over what he could and couldn't eat and could and couldn't do. In short, he was finding it hard to come to terms with the fact that he had had a serious heart attack and was now practically on bed-rest, by order of the doctor. He had played merry hell with the nurses at the hospital and was now intent on torpedoing every single candidate for the job of personal assistant. He flatly refused to use the term 'nursemaid'.

In the meantime, Andreas's life was temporarily on hold. He commuted to his office by private helicopter when his presence was urgently required, but he had more or less taken up residence in the manor house—importing his work to him, communicating via email and conference call, accessing the world from the confines of his godfather's mansion when he was accustomed to being in the heart of the city. Somerset was undeniably beautiful. It was also undeniably inconvenient.

'Getting a little sick of my company, Andreas?'

'Getting a little sick, James, of running into a brick wall every time we interview someone for the job. So far the complaints have ranged from—let's see—"looked too feeble to handle a wheelchair"; "not sufficiently switched on"; "too switched on so wouldn't last"; "seemed shifty"; "personal hygiene problems"; "too overweight"; "didn't click". Not forgetting this latest—"had a moustache".'

'Excellent recall!' James shouted triumphantly. '*Now* you're beginning to see the tricky situation I'm in!' He took a surreptitious swig of his port and eyed his godson to gauge his next move.

'The moustached lady seemed all right,' Andreas observed, ignoring his godfather's smug look at his minor victory in getting his godson to agree that the fifty-five-year-old Ms Pearson might have been a challenging candidate. 'Four more to see tomorrow—but she's on the short list, like it or not.' End of conversation.

Andreas had no doubt that the extremely efficient agency which was currently supplying them with possibilities would lose patience sooner or later, and when that happened he had no idea what he would do.

As it was, the past two weeks had comprised the longest stint he had ever had out of his office, holidays included. Empires didn't run themselves, as he had once told his godfather, and his empire had so many tentacles that controlling them all was an art form that required an ability to juggle work above and beyond the average.

Not that Andreas objected. Brains and talent had seen him cruise through his academic career. Rejecting all offers of help from his godfather, he had left university to embark on his fledgling career in the City. He had moved quickly and effortlessly from the risky trade markets with sufficient capital to set up his own company. Within ten short years he had become a force to be reckoned with in the field of mergers and acquisitions, but when Andreas bought he bought shrewdly and he bought for keeps. Now, in addition to a niche and highly profitable publishing-outfit, he owned a string of first-class boutique hotels in far-flung places, three media companies and a computer company that was right up there in pushing the boundaries of the World Wide Web. He had managed thus far to weave a clever path through the recession, which was revealing gaping inadequacies in companies all over the world; he knew that he was regarded as virtually untouchable. It was a reputation he liked.

Importantly, however, he had never forgotten that the privileged lifestyle which had been donated to him courtesy of his godfather had not been *his.* From a young age he had been determined to create his own privileged lifestyle, and he had succeeded. Everything took second place. Including women—including, in fact, the current one in his life who had recently begun thinking otherwise.

He'd joined his godfather for dinner with his thoughts half on a deal which would net him a very desirable little company in the north which was busy doing some interesting research in the pharmaceutical market. It was one of the few areas in which Andreas had not dabbled, and therefore all the more seductive. But generally his thoughts were on his godfather's stubborn refusal to bow to the inevitable, and the niggling problem of the woman he was currently seeing, Amanda Fellows, who was beginning to outstay her welcome.

'You need to lower your expectations,' Andreas said as dishes were cleared away, and he pushed himself away from the table to look steadily at his godfather, who was beginning to flag. 'You're not going to find perfection.'

'You need to get yourself a good woman,' James retorted briskly. 'Now that we're getting into the arena of giving advice.'

Andreas grinned, because he was used to his godfather's casual disregard for personal boundaries. 'I happen to have a very good woman in tow at the moment, as it happens,' he said, choosing to set aside the debate about the more pressing issue of his godfather's obstinacy because stress was to be avoided above all else, he had been told.

'Bimbo?'

Andreas gave all the appearance of taking time out to consider that. He swirled the wine in his glass around, tilted his head to one side then said, still grinning, 'Who likes brains in a woman? After a hard day's work, the only word I want to hear from any woman is "yes"…'

His godfather bristled predictably, and was in the middle of one of his versions of a 'you need to settle down, boy' rant when the doorbell went.

The doorbell, unlike doorbells on most houses, was the sort of clanging affair that reverberated like church bells inside the house, bouncing off the solid walls and echoing through the multitude of rooms.

* * *

Standing outside, Elizabeth decided that it was the sort of doorbell that perfectly suited the house, which didn't mean that she wasn't jumping with nerves as it announced her arrival. Her finger, in fact, had hovered above it for several minutes before she had finally summoned the courage to press.

The taxi which she could ill afford had dropped her off, circling the vast courtyard, then unhelpfully disappearing back towards civilization—leaving her completely stranded and without much of a clue as to what she was going to do if no one was in.

That was just one of the many things, she now realised, that she had failed to consider.

Indeed, there were so many stomach-clenching 'what if?'s banking up inside her that she had to apply her oft-used technique of breathing in and out very slowly to steady her nerves.

She was in the middle of a deep inhalation, eyes firmly shut, when the door opened and she was confronted by a tiny woman in her sixties with dark hair firmly pulled back into a bun and shrewd, darting eyes.

'Yes?'

Elizabeth swallowed back her trepidation. She had taken ages deciding what to wear. A light flowered dress, her favourite peach cardigan, flat sandals. There wasn't a great deal she could do with her hair, which was long, auburn and always managed to defy any attempts made to control it, but she had tried, tying it back into a long braid that hung down almost to her waist. She looked presentable but it still wasn't enough to instil any self-confidence. She was as nervous now as she had been two months ago when she had first decided on her plan of action.

'Um…I'm here to see Mr Greystone.'

'Appointment?'

'No, I'm afraid not. If it's inconvenient, I could always

come back...' She had noticed a bus stop a couple of miles back. It would be a bit of a hike, but she wasn't going to throw away any more money on calling a taxi. Her fingers played nervously with the leather strap of the handbag over her shoulder.

'Did the agency send you?'

Elizabeth looked blankly at the small woman in front of her. Agency? What agency? Send her for what?

The gaps in her knowledge were beginning to suffocate her. The full extent of everything she knew about James Greystone had been gleaned from the Internet, and she had devoured the information with fascinated interest. She knew what he looked like, how old he was and was aware that he was wealthy—although she had been staggered, on approaching his country mansion, to realise just *how* wealthy he appeared to be. She knew that he had no wife and that he had never had children. She knew that he had retired from the highly profitable construction-business which his grandfather had founded many years previously and was something of a recluse. For someone presumably of some substance, there had been remarkably little about him, and she could only deduce that that was because he had made it his business from early on to keep a low profile.

She knew nothing about any agency. 'Um...' she ventured hesitantly, but it must have been the right response, because the door was drawn back and she stepped into a hallway that took her breath away.

For a few minutes she stood in silence and just stared. Imposing flagstones were interrupted only by an expanse of rug that spoke of generations of use, and directly ahead was a regal staircase that marched upwards before branching out in opposite directions. The paintings on the walls, in their heavy, gilded frames, were of traditional country-scenes and looked as old as the house itself. This house didn't have rooms, it had wings.

Why on earth had she imagined that the best plan of action was direct confrontation? Why hadn't she just done the sensible thing and written a letter, like any normal person would have done in her position?

She snapped back to the present when she realised that the housekeeper had paused at one of the doors and was looking at her enquiringly.

'Mr Greystone is just having coffee in the dining room. If you want to wait here, I'll announce you. Name?'

Elizabeth cleared her throat. 'Miss Jones. Elizabeth Jones. My friends call me Lizzy.'

She waited precisely three minutes and forty-five seconds. Elizabeth knew that because she consulted her watch every few seconds just to try and stop her nerves from spiralling out of control. Then the housekeeper reappeared to show her towards the dining room.

Elizabeth had no idea what to expect. She lost track of the various rooms they passed. When she was finally shown into the dining room, and the housekeeper tactfully did a disappearing act, she realised that she was facing not just James Greystone but someone else, a man with his back to her who was staring out of one of the enormous sash-windows that overlooked the back garden.

She felt her breath catch in her throat as he turned slowly away from the captivating view to look at her.

For a few mesmerising seconds she completely forgot the purpose of her visit. She forgot that James Greystone was sitting right there, metres away from her. She even managed to forget her nerves.

The rich, mellow light from the sun as it began its descent streamed behind him, silhouetting a body that was long, lean and even, clothed in casual trousers and a short-sleeved, open-necked shirt, and highly toned. The man didn't look English, and if he was then there was some other exotic gene in the mix, because his skin was bronzed, his eyes were dark and his hair was raven-black. The chiselled bone-structure was at once beautiful, cold and utterly, bewilderingly magnetic. It took her a few seconds to realise that he was watching her as assessingly as she was watching him, and that James Greystone was watching both of them with interest.

Elizabeth dragged her eyes away, feeling like someone who has been whisked up, around and over on a sudden, thirty-second rollercoaster ride and then dumped back down to earth at supersonic speed.

'Miss Jones… Not sure if you were on the agency's list. Damn fool agency's as incompetent as the day is long…wouldn't be in the least surprised if your name wasn't on it.'

The disturbing sensation of being tumbled about faded as Elizabeth turned to face the reason for her visit in the first place. James Greystone cut an imposing figure with his shock of iron-grey hair, his blue eyes and the easy disposition of a man born into money. He was in a wheelchair, which came as something of a shock. Yet again, there had been this mention of an agency.

Constricted by the presence of the tall, strikingly dominant man by the window, Elizabeth was finding it difficult to get her thoughts in order, never mind rearranging them into something approaching speech. This was definitely not the first impression she had intended to make, gaping like a stranded goldfish.

'CV? Where is it?' Andreas decided to make the first move. This latest offering from the agency seemed to be a nitwit. The girl could barely manage to speak, and she was bright red, clutching her handbag the way a drowning man might clutch at a lifebelt.

'Give the girl a chance to speak, Andreas! This overbearing fellow, by the way, happens to be my godson. You're free to ignore him.'

Ignore him? The advice seemed as futile as telling a swimmer with a bleeding leg to ignore a circling shark, but Elizabeth resolutely turned away from the man and walked hesitantly towards the old man in the wheelchair, still clutching her bag for dear life.

'I'm sorry,' she stammered. 'I'm afraid I haven't brought a CV with me.' She knelt down by the wheelchair so that she was looking up at the old man's lined but still autocratic face. 'You're in a wheelchair. What happened? Do you mind my asking?'

Stunned silence greeted this question, then James Greystone burst out laughing.

'Well, at least you're not afraid of getting to the point! Stand up, girl!' He looked her up and down the way a horse breeder might assess the qualities of possible stock, while Elizabeth's generous heart went out to him.

'I'm sorry,' she whispered. 'You must think me awfully rude. My mother was very poorly for the last two years of her life and she absolutely hated it.'

'Excuse me for breaking up the party…'

From behind her, Andreas's voice was cool and smooth and demanded her attention, even though he had certainly not raised his voice. He walked round to stand behind his godfather and proceeded to give Elizabeth a long, thorough look.

'But,' he said bluntly, 'no CV. Complete mystification at my godfather being in a wheelchair. What exactly *did* the agency tell you, Miss…'

'Jones…Elizabeth.' Mild mannered as she normally was, Elizabeth felt herself get a little hot under the collar, because she just knew that he was fully aware of her name. He obviously was extremely protective about his godfather, didn't like what he saw in her and was arrogant enough to make his feelings known. 'I…I didn't come through the agency.'

'Right. So, let me get this straight. You heard of the job through a friend of a friend of a friend, and decided that you would just pop in and see whether you couldn't get an interview without bothering to go through the hassle of actually making an appointment—am I right?'

He subjected her to the full force of his disapproval and watched, fascinated as she went from shell-pink to white to pink again. She gave every semblance of the innocent girl-next-door, that butter wouldn't melt in her mouth, the 'I only care about helping the needy' type. But Andreas wasn't about to take chances. James was a rich man and rich men attracted gold-diggers; it was as simple as that. At least, with the girls submitted by the agency, stringent background-checks had been made; Andreas had personally made sure to impress the necessity of that upon them. So he wasn't going to be taken in by a chit of a girl who just happened to be passing by and thought she might drop in, on the off chance. No way.

Elizabeth remained silent, her green eyes huge as she worried her lower lip with her teeth.

'Andreas! Stop bullying the poor child.'

Andreas stifled a groan of despair. Trust James to have had something negative to say about every single candidate and then be taken in by the one who had just showed up out of nowhere. 'I'm not bullying her,' he said, keeping his impatience in check, 'I'm trying to establish her credentials.'

'Credentials, predentials! At least this one doesn't come complete with a moustache.'

Elizabeth giggled and then hung her head when Andreas shot her a look of withering disapproval.

'And she seems to have a sense of humour. You, on the

other hand, appear to be losing yours. I like this one. I didn't like any of the others.'

'Be sensible, James.'

'I'm beginning to feel a bit faint, Andreas.' He looked at Elizabeth and spun round his wheelchair so that he was facing her directly. 'You're hired. When can you start?'

'James!'

'Andreas, don't forget what the doctor said about stress; right now, I'm beginning to feel very stressed at your unhelpful attitude. I really think that it's time for me to head to bed. My dear, I would be delighted if you would accept the offer of this job.' He gave her a pitiful smile. 'It's been a dreadful time for me recently. I have been felled by a heart attack and have gone through hell trying to find myself a suitable personal assistant so that I can relieve my godson of the burden of looking after me.'

Elizabeth was amused to see how adroitly he had managed to portray his godson in the least favourable light.

'Of course I'll, er, accept the job offer,' she said shyly, and was thrilled to read genuine relief on the old man's face.

'Right. Andreas will sort out the boring details and I will see you very soon. You've made a feeble old man very happy, my dear.'

He wheeled himself efficiently out of the room; Elizabeth heard him bellowing for Maria and then the sound of scurrying steps. She slowly and reluctantly turned to Andreas. She had contrived to ignore him completely while she had been talking to James Greystone, even though she had been well aware of him, frowning, on the very edges of her perception. Now she was forced to look directly at him, and his impact on her senses was no less now than it had been from the very moment she had first clapped eyes on him.

'So, congrats. You got the job.'

Elizabeth was horribly disconcerted when Andreas slowly circled her in much the same manner as a predator might circle prey before it moves in for the kill.

He moved with the stealthy, economical grace of a tiger, and she very nearly squeaked with dismay when he finally paused to stand directly in front of her.

'Now the interview begins. My godfather might be a pushover, but believe me when I tell you that *I'm* not. Follow me.' He walked away, taking it as a given that she would instantly fall in line, which she did.

'Right.' He turned to face her when they eventually made it to the sitting room, another impressive room with floor-to-ceiling drapes on one wall and on the other a massive fireplace. 'Sit.'

'I wish you'd stop giving orders, Mr…Mr…?'

'Andreas. Keep it firmly planted at the back of your mind.'

'I'm happy to answer your questions.' *Within reason,* Elizabeth thought with a guilty twinge. 'I haven't come here to cause any trouble.'

'Good. Then we should get along just swimmingly. If, however, I discover that you're not what you make yourself out to be, then let me give you every assurance that I will personally see to it that you're strung up and left to dry.'

'That's a horrible thing to say.'

'Consider me a horrible person.'

'Is that how you've dealt with all the people who have applied for this job? By threatening them?'

'All the people who have applied for this job have come down the normal route. They've been vetted to within an inch of their lives by the agency, and they've all had a bucket load of credentials and references to their name. You, on the other hand, swan in here via a friend of a friend of a friend, I'm led to believe. You have no CV, and I'm betting that you're pretty low on the credential-and-reference front as well, but feel free to correct me if I'm wrong.'

Elizabeth had never met a man like this before. To look at, he was spectacular. Everything about him demanded attention, from the physical perfection of his body to the beautiful contours of his harsh face. He was someone who would be noticed in any crowd, anywhere, and she wondered if that was the source of his arrogance. A man like him, accustomed to snapping his fingers and giving orders, would have no time for common courtesy. Right now he was watching her narrowly and she decided that she really, really disliked him.

But he wasn't going to scare her away. It had taken a lot to bring her to this house in the first place; now that she had unexpectedly been offered an opening, she wasn't going to let herself be cowed into leaving.

'Well?' Andreas studied her down-bent head. 'Let's talk about the credentials. Any?' He strode forward, casting a shadow as he towered over her before sitting down on the sofa next to her.

'I'm a qualified secretary,' Elizabeth began, clearing her throat. She'd almost preferred it when he was looming. 'And my boss, Mr Riggs, would provide a very good reference for me.'

'And your job is where, exactly?'

'In West London.'

'Name of company?'

Elizabeth nervously began telling him about what she did at Riggs and Son, which was a small solicitor's office close to the airport, and Andreas held up an imperious hand to halt her in mid-sentence.

'I don't need a complete run-down on the history of the company, and I care even less about Mr Riggs senior retiring. Why would you leave an office job to come and work as a nursemaid to an elderly man?'

It was a very good question and one which Elizabeth was not prepared to answer. However, stuck in the position of having to say something, she mumbled indistinctly about wanting a change.

'Speak up,' Andreas demanded. 'I can't hear a word you're saying.'

'That's because you're making me nervous!'

'Good. Being nervous around me works. Now, enunciate carefully and tell me what's in it for you, taking this post.'

'I…I'm good at looking after people.' She raised her eyes hesitantly to Andreas; he frowned and pushed aside the distracting notion that they were the purest, clearest green he had ever seen. 'I looked after my mum for two years before she died, and I guess some people would find that a chore, but it never bothered me. I liked looking after her. It only seems fair that old people should be taken good care of when they're poorly, and I'm happy doing that.'

'Which beggars the question—why didn't you become a nurse if your Florence Nightingale instincts are so highly developed?'

Andreas's brilliant dark eyes were making her feel disoriented. She knew that, whatever impression she was managing to give, it was the wrong one. She could barely keep still and her face was burning.

'Come on, now, Miss Jones!' Andreas delivered impatiently. 'Get with the program. You're being interviewed, but you can barely string a few sentences together. How am I to think that you're going to be able to handle working alongside my godfather? He might be in a wheelchair, but his intellect is in full, working order. Can you convince me that you'll be able to hold your own when you can barely manage to answer a few simple questions? His food needs to be carefully supervised, he needs exercise on a regular, daily basis.

He enjoys neither of those restraints and is very happy to dig his heels in and refuse to cooperate. Don't you think that he'll be able to run rings around a timid little mouse like yourself? In fact, isn't it all too likely that that's the very *reason* he's so keen on getting you on board?'

Elizabeth felt her temper rise at his flagrant insult. *Timid little mouse?* How dared he just sit there and say whatever he wanted in that lazy, derisive voice of his when he didn't know her?

'Furthermore, you might have won James over by batting those eyelashes of yours and playing the sweet little innocent, but none of that washes with me. As far as I am concerned, you're starting at the baseline point of potential gold-digger.'

'You have no right to accuse me of—'

'I have every right. I'm looking out for my godfather's interests, and from where I'm sitting they don't lie with someone who's walked off the streets with nothing more to her name than a sympathetic expression and a convincing line in blushing.'

Elizabeth summoned up every ounce of courage she possessed and stood up, wishing she had a more commanding height instead of being a mere five-foot three-inches. 'I…I don't have to listen to you. I'm not after your godfather's money. I know you've probably seen loads of really qualified people, but, if Mr Greystone is willing to give me a chance, then I think you should be too.'

'Or else what?'

Elizabeth had no comeback to that sharply spoken question. Her mother had died only recently and she had been allowed extended compassionate-leave from her company, time she had planned to use by venturing down to Somerset so that she could get to meet James Greystone. She had not expected to find him in need of a carer but, now that she had, now that she had been given the chance of actually working for him, the thought of seeing the opportunity snatched out of her hands by the man in front of her filled her with dismay.

'I don't know. Nothing.' Her shoulders drooped in defeat and she stared down at her sandals, wondering whether he had already mentally added 'drab, boring dresser' to his 'timid, little mouse' description of her.

'How did your mother die? She must have been relatively young.'

The change of subject startled her, and Elizabeth looked at him in confusion.

'It's not a trick question, Elizabeth,' Andreas said drily. 'So you don't have to stand there weighing up an appropriate response. Just try and answer the question without looking as though you're being made to walk on a bed of nails.'

Feeling like a parasite spread out on a petrie dish for inspection, Elizabeth stammered into speech. Her mother had battled cancer for two years. She had ignored symptoms for many months because of a fear of doctors and had paid the ultimate price. By the time she had trailed off, Elizabeth's eyes were wet and she rummaged in her bag for a handkerchief, only to find one pressed into her trembling hands.

'I'm sorry,' she mumbled. 'I was very close to my mum and she's… Well, I have no brothers or sisters, and my mum was an only child. In fact, she was adopted, so…'

Andreas swung away from her to walk towards the window. Halfway across the room, Elizabeth was still gulping back her tears while wondering whether to return the soaked hanky to her torturer or tactfully dispose of it in her bag to be laundered and returned at a later date. He had made absolutely no comment on anything she had said, which was not surprising, but what did surprise her was that she was grateful for his silence. She had become weary of facing other people's discomfort and pity.

'Okay,' Andreas said crisply, 'Here's the deal. You get the job, but you're on probation, and don't even *think* of letting it slip your mind that I'll be keeping an eye on you. You'll report to me twice weekly, at the very least, and I will want to see positive progress with my godfather in terms of his exercise routine. James has been writing his memoirs for years. Your secretarial skills will prove useful, so be prepared to use them.'

Elizabeth nodded gratefully, mesmerised, against her will, by the sheer power of his presence. He might be cold, condescending, witheringly derisive and downright insulting, but there was still something impossibly magnetic about him. Once her eyes were on him, it was seductively easy to let them stay there.

The sight of Andreas walking towards her and snapping his fingers yanked her back to reality. 'Hello? Is anybody there? Are you reading me?'

'I'm reading you loud and clear. Sir!'

'Good. Then we're on the same page. My people will be in touch with you tomorrow morning with the contract. Built in will be a one-month probation clause—and that's *my* probationary period, not my godfather's. At the end of that time, you'll either be hired full-time or you'll leave, no questions asked. Understood?'

'Understood.'

'When are you free to start?'

'Immediately,' Elizabeth said, just in case he changed his mind. 'I mean, most of my stuff is still in my bedsit in London.'

'Bedsit? You live in a bedsit? I had no idea that such things still existed.'

Her eyes widened. 'Well, they do, and I live in one of them. I could arrange to get back…let's see…'

'Give me your address. I can have all your possessions

brought to the house by lunchtime tomorrow, and I'll take care of any penalty you incur at your…place of accommodation.'

'Are you sure?'

'Never ask me that question,' Andreas said smoothly. 'I am *always* sure. Where are you staying tonight?'

'A bed and breakfast. It's not fancy, but I couldn't af—'

'No need to elaborate. Be here at ten, sharp, tomorrow morning and bring whatever you have with you. Any questions? No? Good. In that case—' He spun round on his heels and headed to the door '—I'll get Maria to call a cab for you and show you out.'

The door closed quietly behind him and Elizabeth was left feeling wrung out. In fact, she had to sit down, because her legs were threatening to collapse. In none of her wildest daydreams could she have envisaged this scenario but it was all to the good. She closed her eyes and breathed evenly for the first time since she had set foot in the house.

It was a cruel shame that Andreas was to be a fixture on the scene, but that fly in the ointment faded into insignificance next to the impossible slice of good fortune that she was, at long last, going to get to know the father she'd never known about before.

CHAPTER TWO

ELIZABETH had grown up knowing precious little about her father. In fact, practically zero, and she had worked out from an early age that questions on the subject were a no-go area. The 'do not trespass' sign would go up faster than the speed of light. As she had got older, when the other kids at school pressed her for details, asked her whether her parents were divorced, she had shrugged and changed the subject. Divorced parents would have been easy to deal with. Most of her friends had come from divorced backgrounds. Some had had so many marriages and remarriages within the family, and had collected so many half-siblings and step-siblings on the way, that you would have needed a degree in advanced calculus to work it all out.

The only thing she knew for certain about him was that she must have inherited his colouring because her mother had been very blond. Her auburn hair must have come from somewhere.

Then Phyllis had died and every question Elizabeth had mentally asked herself over the years had been answered, thanks to a cardboard box which she had discovered in the attic of her mother's house under the piles of stuff, largely rubbish, which she had had to wade through. There had been letters, some faded pictures and, significantly, a name.

With the help of the Internet, it had taken her under half an hour to learn that her father was alive and kicking and living in Somerset, a widower whose wife had died many years previously.

Putting two and two together, Elizabeth had worked out that Phyllis, at the age of thirty-two, had become the most ordinary of statistics—namely someone who had dated a man and discovered she was pregnant with his child. Had she become the butt of her friends' jokes? Had she had to endure the whispers and sniggers of people who might have been happy to see the blond bombshell brought back down to earth with a bump? People who had gossiped about the woman from the wrong side of the tracks reaching above her station? At any rate, her father had been exorcised from both their lives for ever.

Which didn't mean that Elizabeth still hadn't been curious. Which didn't mean that she didn't want to slot together some of the jigsaw pieces for herself. Armed with concrete information, she had thought long and hard, taken a few deep breaths and made the momentous decision to meet the man she had never known.

She hadn't been entirely sure how exactly she would handle this all-important meeting, but just getting away from west London had seemed a good idea. The time spent caring for her ill parent, whilst working flat out in a frantic effort to keep a rein on the household finances, had drained her of all energy. When Phyllis had eventually passed away, Elizabeth had been a walking zombie. The thought of leaving London and the bedsit into which she had been obliged to move had dangled in front of her like a pot of gold at the end of the rainbow.

The one thing she had known for sure was that she wouldn't barge into her father's house and announce herself as his daughter. Being in the situation in which she now found herself, that had become even more of a certainty for

Elizabeth. Her father was a sick man. The shock of discovering who she was could have untold, dire consequences.

The little batch of incriminating letters lay like an unexploded bomb beneath her underwear in the ornate chest-of-drawers in her bedroom.

The past few weeks had been an exercise in getting to know her father. Despite their wildly different temperaments, they had bonded on a level that was proving to be deeply rewarding. His irascible personality was soothed by her much more even-tempered one, and years of caring for her mother had inured her to the cantankerous demands of the invalid who doesn't want to be the invalid, the only difference being that James was recovering well, whilst her mother had become progressively worse.

It also helped that she was avid in her curiosity about his life, which thrilled him no end, and super-human in her ability to overlook all his faults, so great was her desire to get to know him. Which, likewise, thrilled him to bits.

When to tell him who she really was? No time seemed like a good time. How would he react? Would the shock kill him? She had tried to talk to his consultant about what could happen should something unexpected happen to James, but the conversation had been so convoluted, and the poor man had looked so bemused that she had given up in the end.

If the shock didn't kill him, then would he still want her around? Would he still like her? She was tormented by the notion that he might feel as though she had somehow deceived him, and when she tried to think of how she could explain her decision to him her brain became scrambled and she felt sick.

So Elizabeth dealt with the whole sorry situation by largely pretending that it didn't exist. One day, she vaguely decided, the time would be right, and when that day came she would recognise it and find the courage to do what she was resolutely putting off doing.

With her unease firmly boxed and shoved away for the moment, she walked across to her bedroom window and stared down at a vista of lawns and fields that was breathtaking. For someone who had grown up in the cluttered confines of a neighbourhood where the houses were packed together like sardines in a can, this was a slice of sheer paradise.

Unfortunately, it was a paradise marred by more than just a guilty secret. In fact, she sometimes thought that the guilty secret was nothing compared to Andreas, who was capable of having the most appalling effect on her even when he was in London hundreds of miles away.

She was expected to report to him by email on a daily basis, which was fine, but in addition to the emails there were the phone calls, during which he would cross examine her like a chief inquisitor on the hunt for blood. He asked her questions that were loaded with hidden traps, into which she could inadvertently fall without warning, and made passing remarks that she interpreted as thinly veiled insults. He never forgot to let her know, directly or indirectly, that he was still suspicious of her motives, even if he had trusted her sufficiently to return to his hectic schedule in London.

Elizabeth frowned and walked towards her bathroom. James would be having his siesta, and this was her down time, during which she would have a long, lazy bath and maybe stroll in the garden, read her book or even catch up with some emails; one of the first things presented to her had been a laptop computer.

'It's the fastest method of communication,' Andreas had informed her in his usual scarily cool way. 'I'll expect you to fill me in on my godfather's progress every day. With your own personal laptop, there'll be no room for excuses about forgetting.'

She hadn't cared to think what would happen if she skipped a day, if she forgot. 'Off with her head' sprang to mind.

And then there were his visits.

These were frequent and often unannounced and they always, but always, left her a dithering wreck. Andreas was an expert in making his presence felt in a way that was subtle and invasive at the same time. How on earth did he always manage to find just the question that could stick a pin in her conscience and leave her flustered and hunted? She didn't know, but he excelled at it. Those spectacular dark eyes would lock onto her, she would feel dizzy and faint and then she would babble.

Consequently, she had become adept at avoidance tactics. She would disappear to the town for a spot of shopping, which was something that didn't interest her in the slightest, and reappear just in time to vanish for a bath. She would join them for dinner and would endeavour to keep as low a profile as possible, cringing when James sang her praises, and breathing a sigh of heartfelt relief when she could reasonably excuse herself for bed.

Once the thought of Andreas got into her head, it lodged there like a burr, and not even the luxury of her deep bath could sweep the disturbing images from her mind. Nor was there any image she could super-impose over his. It was as if her disobedient mind had wilfully decided to commit to memory that striking, dark face, those cool, assessing eyes, that wide, sensuous mouth and, once committed, was determined to hold on to the image with ruthless tenacity.

She emerged, warm and flushed, from the bathroom with just her bathrobe around her—and ran slap-bang into the alarming sight of Andreas lounging indolently in her doorway.

It was such an unexpected sight that she had to blink a couple of times because she was convinced that what she was seeing was just a continuation of what she had been thinking only moments before.

The illusion was well and truly shattered when he spoke. 'I knocked.'

Elizabeth went bright red and stared at him until he shook his head impatiently. He walked forward into her room, half-closing the bedroom door behind him, which sent her nerves rocketing into even deeper, helter-skelter frenzy.

'What are you doing here?' she squeaked, following his every movement with trepidation. He was the last person she had expected to see. In fact, he wasn't due a visit until the weekend, two days hence.

Andreas wasn't sure whether to be amused or thoroughly irritated by her obvious dismay. No one could ever accuse the woman of enjoying his company, he thought. In fact, give her a magic wand and he was pretty sure that her first wish would be to make him disappear. But he had knocked, which as far as he was concerned gave him every right to enter when his knock hadn't been answered.

Anyway, this wasn't a social call, and he wasn't about to let her scuttle into hiding until it was safe to emerge, which would be when his godfather came down later for his cup of afternoon tea.

'I've come to see you,' Andreas said smoothly. 'I wanted to get hold of you without James, so I timed my visit to coincide with his siesta. Aren't you flattered?' He looked round the room curiously. 'Would you believe, this is the first time I've been in this particular bedroom? Nice, if a bit heavy on the pastel shades and chintzy fabric. The four-poster bed has Portia's touch written all over it. She had a flair for the showy.' Inspection over, he turned to Elizabeth, devoting every ounce of his attention to her wary, flustered face.

'What do you want?' Elizabeth cleared her throat and tried

very hard to disengage from the reality of her naked body under the bathrobe.

'How are you finding it here?' He walked across to the imposing bay-window and perched on the ledge, his long legs stretched out and loosely crossed at the ankles. 'I mean, we've had innumerable conversations about James and his progress, but surprisingly few about you.'

'You've barged into my bedroom to talk about how I'm enjoying the job?' Elizabeth felt a rare surge of anger, because this was really too much. Did he imagine that she was undeserving of even a modicum of privacy? Did he think that because he had set himself up as her taskmaster that he could do whatever he wanted?

'I didn't barge into your bedroom. I very politely knocked and, when there was no answer, I entered. If you're that obsessive about your privacy, then I suggest you lock your bedroom door as a matter of course.'

'I would have, if I'd known you might have been prowling around,' Elizabeth muttered to the ground.

'But, as a matter of fact, your job satisfaction is only one of a few things I want to talk to you about.'

'The others being…?' She momentarily forgot her embarrassing state of undress, because she couldn't think of anything Andreas might want to chat to her about that was going to be to her benefit. The fact that he had travelled down especially to catch her when James wasn't around sent a shiver of apprehension racing up and down her spine.

'I'm more than happy to have this conversation here,' he drawled by way of response. 'But you might want to get changed and join me in James's office downstairs.'

Which brought Elizabeth right back down to earth at lightning speed. Her fingers tightened on the cord around her waist, threatening to cut off circulation, and she nodded at him tightly.

'And don't even consider stretching it out until James wakes up in two hours' time. Or even gate-crashing his siesta so that he can chaperone you.'

'I wouldn't do that. Don't you think I know how important it is that James has his rest during the day so that he can build his energy back up?'

'Of course you do,' Andreas said in a honeyed voice. 'Although I can't help but notice how much more visible you are when James is around. Almost as though you don't like being in my company. But then that's probably me just being cynical.'

'You *are* a very cynical person,' Elizabeth agreed on a sigh, and Andreas shot her a look of open disbelief.

'I don't suppose anyone ever tells you anything like that, because everyone is so desperate to please you, but you *are* cynical. It's not a very nice trait.' Over the course of time, James had told her about Andreas's girlfriends, or 'blasted airheads', as he liked to describe them. Whilst Elizabeth knew that she shouldn't really indulge in gossip about him behind his back, curiosity had driven her to listen, and what she had learnt had pointed to a guy who played the field with the same ruthless determination as he played the stock markets, always making sure never to stay with one woman long enough for her to get any silly ideas. If that wasn't cynicism, then what was? Even though she had been deprived of the whole two-parent business, and even though she had seen lots of marriages first hand that had ended in tears, Elizabeth still firmly believed in love.

'Not a very nice trait?' Andreas paused on his way out to repeat her frankly spoken remark with incredulity. He had long decided that diplomacy was not one of her more prominent characteristics, but the softly spoken put-down still managed to get under his skin.

'Some people may think it's okay,' Elizabeth told him hurriedly and he raised his eyes skywards with a long-suffering expression.

'I'll expect you in the office in fifteen minutes,' he told her abruptly, not giving her any ghost of an opportunity to latch onto some other random topic which might ambush him into one of those dizzying side roads that her brain seemed to love. He had never met a woman like her. Not only was 'coy' an alien word to her vocabulary, but she could divert him from whatever he happened to be saying with an ease that would have had members of his board gasping with envy.

The last time he had come home, he had casually mentioned over dinner that a dog had almost ended up under the wheels of his Ferrari, only to find himself treated to a disingenuous diatribe on fast cars—which were a threat to other road users, and totally unnecessary, given that a much slower car could easily get a person from A to B without running over poor, innocent animals en route. All counter arguments had fallen on deaf ears, and much to his godfather's vast amusement, he had found himself back on the road, doing thirty miles per hour, searching the roadside to make sure that the dog had in fact escaped an early death.

On certain issues, the shy, blushing maiden was not at all backward in coming forward, he had found.

And yet she continued to be patently awkward in his presence. It was a conundrum which played on his mind a lot more than he cared for.

He would not have been struck dumb with surprise if she had dawdled in her room, against his express instructions, but in fact he heard her timid knock on the door precisely fifteen minutes after he had poured himself a cup of coffee and settled behind the desk in James's grand office.

She had changed into one of her seemingly never-ending

supply of nondescript flowered dresses, which were perfect for the long, warm summer days but incredibly unflattering. This one was shapeless, and over it she wore a very thin cardigan that reached practically down to the tops of her thighs.

'I've printed off your report,' she said, walking hesitantly towards the desk and proferring him two sheets of paper.

'Why would I want to read what you're perfectly capable of telling me yourself face to face?' He gestured to the chair in front of him and then folded his hands lightly on the desk.

'Right. Okay; yesterday James and I went into town. I thought it'd be nice for him. There's a lovely tea shop down one of the side roads, although *naturally* I made sure that he didn't stray from his diet.' She waited for some interruption from him, perhaps reiterating the importance of obeying doctor's orders when it came to James's food intake, but he carried on watching her in complete silence—which was really, really offputting. 'He…he's thinking of joining a bridge club, in fact. One of his friends, a lovely gentleman by the name of—'

'We were going to talk about you,' Andreas smoothly cut in. 'How you're enjoying working for my godfather. You two seem to have clicked. In fact, I hear from him regularly, and it seems that you can't put a foot wrong.'

Elizabeth smiled with real pleasure, and for a few seconds Andreas was distracted into thinking how much that smile lit up her face and transformed her from average to… He frowned and focused.

'It's been absolutely, well, *brilliant* meeting Mr Greystone—James. He's an incredible man. So, if you're asking me how I'm enjoying working here, then I can tell you with my hand on my heart that I'm loving it.'

Andreas held up one imperious hand. 'I get the picture.' He steepled his fingers together and looked at her thoughtfully, his expression shuttered. 'I'll be perfectly honest with you, I didn't think you'd last the month. James is ferociously intelligent and he can be very wilful if he puts his mind to it. He has almost no tolerance for anyone who can't keep up with him, and the fact that he's physically constrained now against his will, the fact that he's in a position of dependency, has made him unbearably short-tempered. I thought you would have been screaming and waving the white flag before you had time to fully unpack.'

'It's worked out very well.' Something about this conversation was making her feel a bit uneasy. He had barely listened to what she had to say about James's recent progress, and yet she found it difficult to imagine that he had made this trip especially to enquire about her. He had had plenty of opportunities to enquire about her, so why start asking probing questions now?

'Yes, I'm very pleased for you. As is Donald Riggs. Remember him? The teddy-bear guy you used to work for once upon a time in west London?' Andreas sat back and watched her carefully, noting the way her eyes flickered past him, then lowered to gaze in apparent fascination at her hands.

'Of course I remember him. I don't understand, though. Why would you have spoken to Mr Riggs? You asked me to provide you with a reference and I made absolutely sure that one was written and posted to you.'

'Yes, and it was all above board. Positively glowing. In fact, I'm surprised they're managing to survive without your fantastic interpersonal skills and great sense of initiative.' He picked up a piece of paper from the desk, which Elizabeth now realised was the requested reference, and read a few sentences that did indeed make her sound like a paragon of efficiency, and all in all an indispensable member of their team.

'Funny thing is, I barely glanced at this reference when it

arrived on my desk a month ago. You had already settled in, James liked you; the reference to all intents and purposes was a formality.' He picked it up and scanned it then handed it to her in silence.

'Go on. Read it and then tell me what you think.'

'I'm very grateful to Mr Riggs for being so kind about me,' she said eventually, having dutifully read and re-read it three times, frowning as she tried to work out what the undercurrent between them was all about.

'Is that all?'

'What else do you want me to say?' Elizabeth asked in confusion. 'Why do you have to play cat-and-mouse games like this? Why can't you just come right out and tell me what you want to say? I know you don't like me, but there's no need to behave like a bully.'

Several things in that statement threatened to send Andreas's blood pressure into orbit, but he wasn't about to be distracted either by what she said or by her enormous, accusing green eyes.

'Reading this,' he said instead, 'Several times over, I got the distinct impression that teddy-bear Riggs assumed you were seeking employment with *me.* Typing speeds, willingness to assume responsibility with important case files, liaising with clients—etc, etc, etc. See where I'm going?'

'Those are the things I used to do in the company. What would you have had him say?'

'Less about the typing speeds, for starters, and a little bit more on the interpersonal skills. In fact, I was surprised typing speeds were mentioned at all, considering you would have asked him for a reference in connection with working for James in the capacity of carer. Hmm. Almost as though teddy-bear Riggs had no real idea about the position for which you were applying. Odd, don't you agree?'

'I'm reliable and efficient. Aren't those the sort of skills you were looking for?'

Andreas ignored that minor interruption. His question had been more of a rhetorical one in nature, not requiring a response. 'Anyway, I thought it might be an idea to get on the phone and have a little chat with the Riggs character.'

Elizabeth didn't say anything. As always with Andreas, what had commenced as a seemingly straightforward question-and-answer session was usually unveiled as a conversational road rife with hidden agendas and cunning traps.

'You're not saying anything. Aren't you interested to hear what he had to say?'

'I know you're going to tell me anyway.'

'True,' Andreas admitted without a hint of apology. 'Now, here's the thing. Your ex-boss had no idea that you were job hunting in beautiful Somerset. You took some leave following your mother's death because you needed to get out of London and there was *something* you had to do in Somerset. He didn't quite specify what this *something* was, but he certainly wasn't under the impression that it involved work. In fact, he was under the impression that it involved *someone,* as opposed to a *something.*'

Now was the time to spill the beans. Now was the time to come clean, to tell Andreas that, yes, she had come to find her father, that she had found him, that the opportunity to get to know him as herself rather than as an estranged daughter had been irresistible. It would be good, wouldn't it, to confess everything?

In her mind's eye, she pictured Andreas and his reaction. He was not a man given to half measures nor, for that matter, seeing things in shades of grey. Life was a black-and-white business for him. Avoidance of truth would not be construed as a sensitive approach to a delicate situation; it would be seen as an ungovernable lie fit for the most severe of punishments.

And would he see fit to tell James the truth? Or would he, like her, not want to risk his health by being the harbinger of such shocking news? Would he just chuck her out? Maybe tell her to wait until James was fully recovered? If he did, then how long would she have to wait?

Elizabeth would never have thought it possible that she could build such a strong connection with the man whose presence in her life had always been in her imagination. She could never have hoped that their personalities would have clicked so smoothly. Having found that they did, her desperation to hang on was overwhelming.

Into the breach of her silence, as she wrestled with the sudden onslaught of conflicting consequences, Andreas said in a deadly smooth voice, 'How on earth would you have heard about this placement in London—and, if you had, then why the secrecy? Why not just tell teddy-bear Riggs that you needed a change of scenery, that you wanted to pursue a different career?'

'I… You're confusing me.'

'Then spill the beans. Tell me what you're doing here. Really.'

'I…I…' Elizabeth pressed the palms of her hands against her face and took a deep breath. 'I *did* want a change of scenery—from everything—and, yes, I came here on the off chance of meeting your godfather because… Because you're wrong—I *had* heard of him.' Strictly speaking, none of that was untrue, but still she felt horrible at having to fiddle with the truth and pull it to bits and pieces so that she could pick and choose which bits she wanted and which bits she didn't.

'I didn't want to tell Donald, Mr Riggs, anything because I wasn't sure whether I would need to go back to my old job or not. I had to keep my options open. When I asked him to supply a reference, I guess I didn't mention details of the job. In fact, I didn't actually speak to Donald at all. He was in a meeting, and I spoke to Caroline. I don't know her very well, because she joined a month before I left, so I just told her the basics—that I had found employment down here. I gave the address you gave me and asked her to pass the message on that you needed a reference from Donald.'

'Why do I get the feeling that there's something important missing from this narrative?'

'Because you're suspicious by nature. Because you're never, ever willing to give anyone the benefit of the doubt.' Her heart was beating so hard that she wanted to put her hand to her chest to steady it. Instead, she clasped her fingers together on her lap and waited for the axe to fall. The prospect of being flung out on her ear without explanation—or the chance to explain everything to James and then being prepared to take the consequences, whatever they might be—was just too much. She squeezed her eyes tightly shut and chewed on her lip, willing herself not to be a weakling and cry. Andreas would detest weaklings. He would probably chuck her out just for showing emotion.

Unfortunately, her head was in no mood to listen to reason, and the trickle of tears felt cool against her hot, flushed skin.

'Sorry,' she mumbled thickly.

Andreas watched this display of emotion with a censorious frown, at a loss as to what to make of it. On the one hand, he was a gut believer in his own instincts, which were positively screaming that something in the picture wasn't right. On the other hand, he was capable of recognising genuine feeling when he saw it, and there was nothing staged about this bout of waterworks—and he had seen a fair amount of female waterworks in his time. The tap, he had long recognised, could be switched off at the drop of a hat. This tap, however, looked as though it might continue leaking indefinitely. He stood up and circled the desk so that he could hand her his handkerchief, which she took without looking at him, although he thought he heard a muffled, 'Sorry.' He perched on the desk, staring at her down-bent head with a perplexed frown, until she had gathered herself.

'I'm not a monster. I do sometimes give people the benefit of the doubt.' He tried to think of the last time he had done so and couldn't.

Elizabeth raised hopeful eyes to his and said, with earnest urgency, 'I would never do anything to hurt James. I'm not here to take advantage of an old man. I know that's what's going through your head.'

'You have no idea what's going through my head.'

'I know it won't be good.'

'You're being ridiculous.'

'I'm just asking you to trust me when I tell you that I'm not a gold-digger. I don't care about money.'

'Even though you've never had any?'

'I know it's a cliché, but money doesn't buy happiness.'

'I have no idea how we managed to get into this conversation.' Andreas stood up abruptly because those wide, green eyes were threatening to do something to his legendary cool. 'I'm prepared to give you the benefit of the doubt in this instance because dispatching you might do more damage to my godfather than keeping you on. He's taken to you, and this is a challenging time in his life. I don't know what might happen if we have to go through the nuisance of trying to find a substitute, especially if no real explanation's given for the vanishing act.'

Elizabeth smiled tremulously and reached out to take hold of his hand, releasing it when he glanced down with a look of mingled surprise and displeasure. 'You won't regret it.'

'You bet I won't, and here's why.' He had given this a great deal of thought. Had she confessed to some sinister, ulterior motives, he would have had no option but to sack her on the spot, but he knew that that had been an unlikely possibility. In which case, hustling her through the back door and then trying to fabricate a plausible explanation for his godfather would be nigh on impossible. Which left him no option but to be in a position from which he could seriously keep an eye on her. Emails and phone calls, whilst helpful, could not even be loosely categorised as seriously keeping an eye on her. She could be using her free time to rummage through bank-account details, for all he knew!

He very firmly neutered the little voice in his head telling him that that was a preposterous suggestion. Since when was he the sort of guy who fell for a woman's tricks? Or anyone else's, for that matter? Life at the very summit of the food chain had opened his eyes to the folly of taking people at face value.

He circled her and then paused to look down at her very carefully, taking in the anxious, heart-shaped face, the softly parted lips, the big, innocent eyes still glistening from her crying jag.

'I'm coming back home.'

CHAPTER THREE

'COMING back home?' Elizabeth was utterly bewildered. Didn't he live in London? 'Don't you live in London?'

'Keep up here, Elizabeth. I'm moving back down to Somerset.' He had resumed his seat at the desk and was tilting back in it, hands folded behind his head, his dark eyes gleaming with satisfaction. The whole upheaval should have been a major source of dissatisfaction for him. His office was the throbbing soul of his operations, and the thought of being plucked out of it for reasons not of his choosing should have set his teeth on edge, but he felt strangely content with the decision.

'You're moving back down to Somerset.' She could scarcely believe her ears.

'You seem to be in a state of shock.'

'You're moving back down to Somerset so that you can watch my every move. You said that you were going to give me the benefit of the doubt.'

'And I have. Which is why you're still in gainful employment!'

Elizabeth looked at him reprovingly and fumbled with the handkerchief which she was still clutching. 'You would jeopardise your whole working life just because you think that I'm here to do I don't know what?'

'I'm not jeopardising anything,' Andreas refuted smoothly. 'I worked here perfectly fine when James returned from hospital. It's a big house and, convenient though it is to be in an office environment where everyone is on hand, keeping in touch is really only the press of a button. The joys of the World Wide Web! Some of my employees actually design their own working hours to incorporate working from home. I'm a very progressive employer.'

Elizabeth was lost in her own tangled thoughts. How on earth was she going to avoid him when he planned on being around all the time, watching her every move? Would he follow her into town when she went to do the shopping? Lurk outside her bedroom with his ear pressed to a glass against the door to find out what she was up to? She imagined bumping into him at unexpected moments, or turning corners to find him lying in wait like a big-game hunter waiting to pounce. She shuddered and realised that he had been saying something.

'I beg your pardon?'

'That's going to have to change, for a start.'

'What are you talking about?'

'I'm talking about your habit of not listening to me when I speak to you.' Or else responding with the briefest of answers and with the general demeanour of someone who would prefer to be anywhere in the universe except in his company. Both traits irritated the hell out of him.

Elizabeth blinked, but, really, how surprised should she be? Andreas resided in a different hemisphere from most other people. In his rarefied world, he snapped his fingers and everyone saluted and jumped to immediate attention.

'I do listen,' she told him. 'I was just thinking about how awkward it's going to be if you're following me around every second of the day…'

'Why would I be following you around every second of the

day?' Andreas asked, his darkly handsome face incredulous at the suggestion. 'I may be prepared to transfer operations down here for the foreseeable future, but I don't intend to abandon work completely so that I can stalk your every movement.'

Foreseeable future?

'You can't migrate here for the foreseeable future,' she said in a staggered voice. 'Don't you have to run your empire?'

'We're not talking about a pirate ship here,' Andreas told her drily. 'There won't be mutiny if I'm not clocking in on a daily basis.'

'Yes, but...'

'Apologies for pointing out the obvious, but that look of horror on your face isn't doing your "give me the benefit of the doubt" cause any good.'

'I'm horrified at the thought of you being around all the time!' Elizabeth blurted out with brutal truthfulness. 'I don't like you. You make me nervous. Of course I'm not going to look forward to you moving in.'

Andreas gritted his teeth in the face of this level of blunt honesty. 'Liking me isn't a requirement,' he imparted grimly. 'In fact, *not* liking me would work very well for the situation I have in mind. However, reacting like a cat on a hot tin roof every time I talk to you isn't going to do.'

Elizabeth couldn't really imagine why someone would not want to be liked; it seemed the most basic and natural of human desires. But then Andreas wasn't like everyone else, was he? 'For the situation you have in mind?' She looked at him blankly and waited for whatever new and disturbing revelation he had to relay.

'I wondered when you would clock on to what I just said.' He sighed elaborately, picked up James's fountain pen which was lying on the desk and twirled it ruminatively between his fingers before transferring his gaze to her expectant face.

'The wonders of Internet access only really go so far,' he explained ruefully. 'Nothing really replaces the good, old-fashioned secretary. Someone to file reports, fend unwanted phone calls, take notes, bring those essential cups of coffee...' He paused, allowing that lazy observation to sink in and take root. 'Which is where *you* come in.'

'No.'

'Oh, but yes.' He dropped the pen and angled her a brooding, speculative look. There was so much that had his antennae on red alert, from that phone call to her ex-boss, to her evident alarm at the thought of him being around. Yet, if she did have something to hide, wouldn't she be acting a little less distracted? If, as he had gleaned from reading between the lines, she had headed to Somerset with the express intention of meeting James, of edging her foot through the door and then hunting down the family jewels, wouldn't she be playing it cool?

Gold-diggers came in all shapes and sizes, admittedly, but they were universally manipulative, cunning and opportunistic. They didn't spend hours browsing through junk shops with a cantankerous seventy-something, as he had gathered she had been doing from the various communications with his godfather over the weeks. They didn't reject their host's offers of having every meal catered to the highest standard in favour of trying out home-cooked food from the antiquated recipe-books James had stored in various cupboards in the kitchen. Nor did they spend their leisure time with the head gardener chatting about plants or else sitting in the walled garden with a book. That took cunning to an altogether new level, and one that Andreas had difficulty getting his head around.

Which was not to say that he didn't feel compelled to oversee the situation. It never paid to take anything in life for granted, and that included the rest of the human race.

'I can't work for *you.* I work for Mr Greystone. I know you insisted that I answer to you, but at the end of the day…'

'Let's think out of the box for a minute. Yes, you do work for James, and from what I gather you're the perfect companion—by which, I take it, you have inordinate reserves of patience. Apparently there was a fracas at the tea shop because the scones advertised had sold out?'

Elizabeth momentarily forgot her stress and gave him one of those radiant, transforming smiles. 'Oh, did he mention that to you?'

'Apparently he spent so long arguing with the manager about their policy of leaving the board up when the scones were no longer available that he's been given a voucher for free teas there for the next fortnight.'

'He *did* huff and puff about never darkening their doors again, but of course he will. He says they do the best cream-teas in the county—even if he can't have the cream—and, besides, I think he likes Dot Evans. She told him to stop spluttering because it wasn't good for his blood pressure, and that if he kicked up a scene in her shop again she would drag him out to the kitchen and force him to do the dishes.'

Andreas was temporarily derailed by the first part of her remark. '*Likes* Dot Evans? Don't be ridiculous. He's known the woman for the past ten years! Don't you think I would have known about it by now?'

'I guess so,' Elizabeth backtracked vaguely, shifting her gaze away and waiting in silence for him to return to the thorny subject of her impending doom.

'Not so fast.'

'Excuse me?'

'Don't you think I've noticed that tendency you have to fall silent the minute a conversation gets a little awkward?' Yes, spot on. He had read her correctly, judging from the sudden bloom of colour on her cheeks. Well, at least his ability to read women hadn't been completely turned on its head in her case.

'I don't like talking about things James might have said. Or not said. Okay—said. When he's not here to…um…say it himself.'

'What?'

'Nothing.'

'What did my godfather say? You're kidding about Dot Evans, right?' His ebony brows knitted into a perplexed frown. He knew Dot Evans, of course. She had been a fixture of sorts on the scene for the past ten years, when James had loaned her money to set up the tea shop in the village. In actual fact she and James had been classmates at school a hundred years ago. He couldn't remember her visiting the house, though. Or had she? Andreas had tried over time to visit his godfather as much as humanly possible, but the frantic pace of work had often waylaid the best thought-out plans. It was easy for things to be left unsaid when visits were snatched.

'It's just a feeling I get.'

'And how is that I've been kept in the dark about this? You're not breaking some secret code by telling me, so you might as well come clean.'

Elizabeth hesitated. Nothing said to her had ever been said in confidence. Although James could be belligerent, forthright and opinionated, he could also be endearingly diplomatic. Diplomacy had prevented him from telling his godson about Dot because when it came to the opposite sex he and Andreas were miles apart. He might have had an affair with her mother, but from what she had gathered about his ex-wife it had been a response to a loveless marriage. Of course, he had never mentioned a word about ever having had a mistress, but the more she knew him the more she realised that he was, essentially, a man of honour.

Would he have ended his marriage for Phyllis? She didn't think so, but it was a question that could never be answered, because her mother had scarpered the second she had discovered he was married, taking the secret of her pregnancy with her. It was tempting to play with the fantasy of wondering what her life might have been like if James had been a free man, had been able to pursue her mother and marry her.

Lost in her day dreams, she started when Andreas snapped his fingers and delivered her a censorious frown.

'You'll be astounded to hear this, but most women don't drift off into never-never land when I'm trying to have a conversation with them!'

'Sorry.'

'He must be ashamed of her,' Andreas mused. 'Can't understand why, unless it's a money thing, although James has never been a snob.'

'Of course he's not ashamed of Dot Evans. She's a lovely lady. He just doesn't think that you…' The words were halfway out of her mouth before she realised that she had uttered them, and she was mortified when Andreas fixed her with his brilliant dark, questioning eyes.

'Carry on. I'm intrigued to find out where this is leading. Do you know that you have a talent for getting me off-topic?'

'I'm not sure he has much time for…for some of the women you go out with,' she said in a rush. 'So…'

'So why bother to mention any lady interest in his life when we don't talk the same language?' Andreas finished for her and she nodded, chewing her lip nervously. Generally speaking, the opinions of other people had virtually no effect on Andreas. However, his godfather was the exception. Yet, instead of feeling hurt that in this one important area of his life James sincerely felt that he could not confide in him, Andreas was reluctantly forced to concede that he had a point.

He thought of Amanda, with whom he had yet to break off, although it was overdue. Amanda, the leggy catwalk-model with not much of a line in intelligent conversation but a killer body and head-turning looks. She was just the latest in a procession of clones and, whilst that worked perfectly for him, it couldn't be said that his godfather understood.

'Of course,' Elizabeth broke in hurriedly, 'it's all about live and let live.'

'Your own personal theory, or another of James's quotes?'

'It's just that he doesn't understand why you go out with the women you go out with.' From the frying pan into the fire, she thought.

'I didn't come down here to have a heart to heart with you about my private life,' he bit out grittily, determined to drag the conversation back to the place from which it should never have strayed to start with. 'We need to sort out the nuts and bolts of you working for me—and there's no point weeping and wailing and wringing your hands. I'm not going to take you away from your duties to my godfather, but I have gleaned that he's recovering fast.'

Elizabeth nodded, resigned to her fate.

'And your afternoons are pretty much your own anyway, when he has his siesta?'

She nodded again, her thoughts now on what working for Andreas might entail. She didn't think that he could be anything but a cruel taskmaster, whatever his claims about being a progressive employer. He would be far from progressive when it came to dealing with a potential gold-digger, which was what he thought she might be. In fact, being the caveman might be more his approach to the situation.

Belatedly, she realised that her mind had again wandered, and she focused on Andreas. It was an unsettling experience, as it always seemed to be. Sometimes in the past he had arrived by helicopter, descending from the sky like a dark, threatening hawk determined to disrupt the peaceful routine of her life. This time, however, he had come by car. She had spotted his sleek, shiny, testosterone-fuelled sportscar in the courtyard on the way to the office, yet he certainly didn't look like someone who had spent hours on the road. In fact, he looked as cool as the proverbial cucumber, in his cream trousers and pale-blue shirt that seemed to emphasise the stunning bronzed colour of his skin.

The top two buttons of his shirt were undone, and as she glanced away from the little glimpse of chest her eyes collided with his strong, muscled forearms and became riveted to the way his fine, dark hair curled around the gold band of his watch. His mega-expensive watch. A mega-expensive watch for a mega-wealthy guy—which brought her back to the whole point of his appearance on the scene. The rich protected their own, and it was galling to think that she had been cast in the role of interloper.

'I try to catch up on my emails when James has his afternoon nap. Sometimes I potter in the garden.'

'Yes. I know. Recent communications from James have shown you have a touching interest in horticulture. Emails to whom?'

'Friends. I've always made a big effort to keep in touch with people who've left London and gone abroad to live. Or maybe just left for the country. Some have.'

'Boyfriend?'

Elizabeth flushed. 'No. Is this relevant?'

Andreas didn't answer, although he was curious to press for more details on the subject of the absence of a man in her life. He figured that her reticence in revealing anything at all about her life must have sparked his curiosity. Only natural. And, even if she insisted on wearing outfits that looked as though they had been rescued from a charity shop, there was a body under there—although what it was like he had no idea, because she was an expert at covering it up. Full breasts; he knew that. Obeying the direction of his thoughts, his eyes drifted down to her breasts, which were more than a generous handful, and shapely. He wondered what they looked like, and slammed the door shut on those inappropriate thoughts.

'Everything is relevant,' he said shortly. 'Remember that and we'll be working on the same wavelength. I'm happy for you to spend the morning with James, but between the hours of one-thirty and five I will expect you to work for me. Sometimes you may be needed to work overtime, and we can discuss that as and when those occasions occur.'

'Overtime?'

'Your ex-boss said that there was never a problem with that until the end, when you obviously needed to spend progressively more time with your mother.'

'I will need to have time for myself,' Elizabeth ventured. 'I enjoy walking into the village sometimes…'

'Which is what weekends will be for.' He leaned forward, his arms on the desk, and gave her a reproving look.

'You're onto a pretty good deal here, and let's not forget that. I don't know exactly why you chose to come here, and for the moment I can't do anything about that—but you're here now, and from where I'm sitting you've landed yourself a nice, cushy number. You're being paid roughly twice as much as you were getting in London for a job that's, probably, roughly half as demanding. Naturally, once you start working for me, you'll be additionally compensated.'

He named a figure that made her gasp.

'I—I couldn't,' she stammered, and Andreas frowned at her.

'Why not?'

'Because it's too much.'

He narrowed his eyes on her flushed face, but when she looked at him it was with total sincerity. 'You don't want the money because you think you'll be overpaid? How crazy is that?' For some reason, he really didn't think it was a case of double bluff. It was hard work constantly reminding himself that nothing and no one should ever be taken at face value. James was worth a considerable amount of money, and while Andreas had absolutely no claim to a penny of it, having insisted a long time ago that he be written out of his godfather's will, he was still intent on making sure that none of it fell into the wrong hands. A less likely candidate for those wrong hands was the woman who had just tried to refuse a pay increase. Did that make sense?

'I'd stay here with James even if I weren't being paid,' Elizabeth told him truthfully. In fact, she was dutifully putting most of the money she earned into a separate account, which she had opened up on one of her days off. She wasn't sure why, but touching as little of the money as possible alleviated some of her guilt at accepting it in the first place. Maybe when she finally told him who she really was she would make a symbolic gesture and return all the money to him. She didn't want to think about it. The longer she stayed, the steeper the hill she had to climb seemed. What would her father say? He was getting stronger by the day, yet she continued to postpone the inevitable, telling herself that the time was not quite right. When she hadn't known him, when curiosity had been her only driving emotion, she had been a lot less scared than she was now.

'So please don't give me any more money,' she finished lamely. 'What would I do with it, anyway? I mean, it's not as though I'm into expensive clothes or jewellery or stuff like that.'

Andreas hesitated. There were practical things to discuss. He would have to familiarise her with the systems which he already had in place on his computer. A high-speed desktop was to be delivered and installed by the end of the day. Everything necessary to transform one of the sprawling and unused rooms on the ground floor would be put into place within the next three hours. He would need her there so that she could have first-hand experience of the layout.

'I find that hard to believe. *All* women are into clothes and jewellery.' His dark eyes did a comprehensive once-over of her body. 'Okay, so maybe not *all*. Which makes me curious—what did you spend your money on? You weren't badly paid in that last job of yours. Hell, you must have a tidy little sum stashed away for a rainy day.'

Elizabeth hesitated. She dearly wanted to tell him that her personal finances were no business of his, but politely backing off was not Andreas's style. Also, now that he was on a self-confessed witch-hunt, determined to prise her open like a walnut and poke around until he found whatever he was looking for, being unnecessarily secretive would only fire him up.

'I have some savings, but not very much,' she told him carefully. 'Mum had to give up her job when she became ill. At first the company was very understanding, but they were a small business and they couldn't afford to keep on paying her when she began taking so much time off work. And then she became weaker, and even going in between the hospital visits was too much, so there was only my income to rely on.'

'Isn't there a benefits system that covers this sort of thing?' It didn't take a massive leap of the imagination to work out that, but for fate and the benevolent guiding hand of his godfather, he might well have ended up in the position of being up close and personal with all the services a welfare state could provide. Since her story of penury was just something else to be factored in to a hidden agenda, however, he refused to allow that pull of sympathy to blinker him.

'Mum was very proud. She would never have taken a penny

from the state, which meant that really all my earnings were spent on the essentials. Whatever was left over, I used to buy mum little treats. She enjoyed going to the shops. In fact, I think I might have been a bit of a disappointment to her, because I never did. I can remember her trying hard to get me involved in clothes and fashion, but I was always much more of a bookworm. In fact, I would have liked to go to university, but of course that was impossible, given the circumstances.'

Where the hell had all that come from? 'So, you see, I don't have any money stashed away for a rainy day.' She could have added that she had been so broke by the time the funeral expenses had been paid that there had been no way that she could carry on renting the three-bedroomed house she had shared with her mother. Not that she would have chosen to.

'Which I guess makes me a potential gold-digger, if not having a lot of money is the only requisite.'

'Go to university—to do what?'

Elizabeth blinked in confusion. 'To study law,' she told him awkwardly. 'I might not have been clever enough, though,' she confessed, which reminded Andreas that this was not the conversation he had intended to have when he had driven down to Somerset. In fact, girlish outpourings of confidence were the last thing he needed, and something he strived hard never to encourage in anyone.

'Running yourself down is counter-productive,' he asserted briskly. 'We can all do whatever we set out to do, or we can slouch around moaning and whingeing and blaming the rest of the world for our own lack of get up and go.'

'I never blame anyone for what happens in my life.'

'Did I refer to you? I was generalising.'

Elizabeth was tempted to tell him that it was all right for *him* to sit there in all his arrogant perfection and lecture about other people's lack of get up and go but then knew that she would sound precisely like the kind of whingeing, blaming person he had just criticised. And, since it looked as though they would be working together for at least part of the day, every day for the *foreseeable future,* it was probably not such a good idea to get off on an even worse footing than they already had.

But he really was perfect, wasn't he?

Her eyes surreptitiously crept to the forbidding set of his dark, hard features. Cold and ruthless he might be, but he was drop-dead gorgeous, and just mentally admitting that reality kick-started a reaction in her body that made her tense in dismay. Her nipples tightened in her bra, and there was a hot ache that started in her belly and seemed to explode into every nerve-ending in a horrible starburst-effect.

'James might object to this arrangement,' she said suddenly.

Andreas squashed that faint hope before it had time to take root. 'I've already run the idea past him, and you'll be overjoyed to know that he has no problem with it. In fact, he sounded delighted. Maybe he's concerned at all those wasted hours during the day when you're stuck on your own with nothing to do but relax.'

Back to the level playing-field with which she was accustomed, Elizabeth lowered her eyes and stared down at the ground in resentful silence, broken only when Andreas restively rose to his feet and walked towards the door.

'Right. No time like the present. My people will be in shortly, and I want you to familiarise yourself with your new office. Follow me.'

He talked while he walked, expecting her to keep up with him. This was the interview she had never had, but then getting the job with James had not required detailed knowledge of computer systems and programs, spreadsheets, budget reports, and data bases. She would, he informed her baldly, be barred from access to any confidential information, but she would need to settle in fast so that she could begin the process of sifting through the hundreds of emails that arrived daily for him, making sure that he didn't waste his valuable time on rubbish.

'I've only had experience working in a small family-firm of lawyers,' she said nervously, tripping along behind him and nearly colliding into him when he stopped abruptly and turned to face her.

'Meaning?' Andreas's voice was cool and lacked encouragement. He had already fallen victim to being sucked in by her timid conversational forays that had nothing whatsoever to do with the matter in hand.

'Meaning that I'm really not sure that I'll be up to your… your high standards.'

'There you go, running yourself down again.'

'I'm not running myself down! I'm being realistic.' But he was off again, and he was so much taller than she was that she had to practically run to keep up.

She also wanted to talk to him about James. Had he given his blessing to this weird arrangement because he thought that she was taking advantage of her position, lounging around doing nothing during all those long afternoons when he was resting?

She was in a state of heightened tension by the time they made it to one of the rooms on the far side of the house, which had the attractive feature of being surrounded by garden on two sides.

His timing was impeccable, because no sooner had they reached the room than a clutch of men were ushered in and the transformation from sitting room to state-of-the-art office began in earnest. Men in white overalls began expertly clearing the room of furniture, working quickly and efficiently like little ants, while Andreas spoke in a low, clipped voice to a guy in a suit who kept pointing to various electrical outlets and scanning down a sheet of paper with lots of designs and scribbles all over it.

Eventually, Andreas led her to the room next door, sat her down and flipped open his laptop.

'You will automatically receive all the emails sent to me on my three business-addresses.' He began booting up the computer while she watched and wondered how she was going to keep up with him.

'What did James tell you?' she asked on a nervous whisper, hardly registering that she had intended to ask that question. Seeing the perplexed frown on his face, she elaborated, 'Does he think that I'm taking advantage of him, relaxing when I should be working? I do often dabble on his book when he's resting. Also, I like to hunt down cookery books in the kitchen. Now and again, I prepare stuff I think he'd like…'

'Why does it matter what James thinks of you? You're being paid handsomely.'

'Of course it matters,' Elizabeth told him in a pained voice. 'And, I told you, I don't care about the money.'

'He doesn't think you're a time waster. Good enough answer? Ready to get down to business?' He looked at his watch, then very quickly began accessing various accounts, while she frantically wrote notes on a pad until her hand began to hurt. Every so often, he asked her if she had any questions, but his voice didn't give her any warm, furry feeling that he would hold her hand while she found her feet. The opposite, in fact. By the time he stood up and flexed his muscles, she felt as though she had been put through the mill.

'I should warn you in advance,' Andreas said, 'That I don't have a great deal of patience for people who can't keep up with me.'

Elizabeth sighed, rotating her wrist gently in the hope that it might ease the soreness of her aching muscles. 'I wonder why that doesn't surprise me? I've never in my life met anyone as impatient as you.' She began gathering the copious notes she had taken, which would now replace her light detective-novel as her bedtime reading. 'But this wasn't part of the deal when I took the post of working for James,' she felt constrained to point out, even though his disapproving dark eyes were threatening to halt her in mid-sentence. 'So you're going to have to curb your impatience.'

'I'm going to have to *curb my impatience?*'

'Yes. You are.' She refused to be cowed by the disbelief stamped on his face. She could very easily foresee him trampling her into the ground without the ghost of a conscience. Soft she might very well be, but not so soft that she would allow him to ruin the precious time she had with her father. Maybe his plan was to drive her away by making her life a living hell. If that was the case, then it was as well that she stood up for herself now.

'And furthermore,' she continued, squaring up for his responding attack, 'I'll work for you, but *only* when James is having his afternoon nap. I won't be badgered into the occasional morning because you have something that needs doing faster than the speed of light, and I won't be forced to work overtime because you're a workaholic and don't know when to stop. As soon as the clock strikes, I quit, even if it means switching off the computer in the middle of typing a sentence.'

'That's an admirably responsible approach to work.' But he was taken aback by the outburst, and intrigued to find that he was looking at her without the usual surge of anger that might have been expected considering his instructions were being questioned.

'I am very responsible when it comes to James, and I'll be very responsible for you, provided you don't try to take advantage of me.'

Poor choice of words. That set up another link in his head that he was in no mood to enjoy.

'So,' he mused thoughtfully, 'I knew there had to be more to you than the meek-and-mild little mouse who scuttled away every time I came too close.'

'I'm just trying to stand my ground.'

'No wonder you've managed to make a roaring success of this job. I bet poor James doesn't know who calls the shots! You use a soft voice and he probably doesn't even notice that you're getting him to do exactly what you want.'

There was an element of truth in that, certainly when it came to restricting James's diet according to doctor's orders and making sure that he took regular exercise. But was there also the implication in Andreas's softly spoken remark that she was manipulative?

'But soft voices don't work on me,' he drawled. 'And I have yet to meet anyone who can get me to do exactly what they want. So, now that we've both cleared the air, let the fun begin.'

CHAPTER FOUR

ELIZABETH looked at her reflection in the mirror and tried to impose order on the host of questions in her head clamouring for answers. Question one centred on her clothes and the fact that over the past three weeks, ever since she had started working for Andreas, she had morphed from comfy to business, even though there was absolutely no need. It wasn't as though she was actually working in an office occupied by other people, where important clients might pop in and question the efficiency of a company with a slack dress-code. But she had felt uncomfortable sitting at her desk, which was adjacent to Andreas's, wearing tracksuit bottoms and sneakers. So on day three she had worn a skirt, some fairly respectable black pumps and a white tee-shirt—and she had caught something in his eyes as they had flickered over her, even though he had said nothing. That something, gone before it had appeared, had stirred something inside her, and she had found herself thinking more and more carefully about her outfits. She knew it wasn't healthy but she just couldn't seem to help herself.

Even James, whose two pet hates were the tabloid press and fashionista airheads, had made a big deal about her snappy appearance when he had happened to exit his bedroom just as she was poised to descend the grand staircase the day before. He had cackled with laughter, wondered aloud where his little helper had gone and then made a great song and dance, pretending to look for her. She had been wearing a pair of olive-green trousers yesterday, bought only the week before, and a pale-green shirt that reflected the colour of her eyes.

Today, she was back in her grey skirt, but with a duck-egg-blue collared tee-shirt—another new item. All this, she told herself firmly, because it was easier to be professional around Andreas if she dressed the part. Otherwise, his bullet-like commands, his frequent, uninvited forays into her private life, and his soaring impatience with any sign of hesitation when it came to the relentless onslaught of work that she faced for those few, snatched hours during the day, would have reduced her confidence to pulp.

Working clothes were her uniform and her mask, and they allowed her to become the super-efficient secretary she had previously been in her last job instead of the dithering wreck she had become in Andreas's presence. So it made sense to tailor her trips to the town with the purpose of buying suitable work-wear. It had nothing to do with inviting his attention because his attention was never on her.

Question two involved the gradual stretching of her hours. Of course, her mornings still belonged to her and James, but recently he had joined a bridge group with Dot Evans and a couple of old friends, who had managed to persuade him that he would mummify if he didn't leave the house occasionally and return to his old routines. They met twice a week at five in the evening, and on those days she had found herself staying on with Andreas, even though she had made such a fuss about sticking religiously to the hours upon which they had agreed. She didn't mind. In fact, she was dangerously aware that she was becoming accustomed to the high-octane pace of working alongside him. When he sat back and glanced at his watch, and told her in that lazy, dry drawl that she was free to leave, it was as though she had crash-landed back on earth after a thrilling ride in a hot-air balloon.

She wouldn't have breathed a word of that to another living soul. It was her secret, those weird feelings she got whenever she was around Andreas.

She timed her arrival today precisely for two, knocking on the door and pushing it open when she was imperiously told to enter.

It still irked her that Andreas could remain the archetypal boss, in total command whatever the clothes he was wearing. Today, he was in a pair of khaki trousers and a faded tee-shirt, and he gave a bark of dry laughter as he took in the expression on her face as she looked at him.

'Dress code not quite in order?'

Elizabeth sat at her desk and swivelled in her chair so that she was facing him. She was no longer quite as intimidated by his mocking sarcasm, which could only be dealt with by remaining calm and unruffled.

'You're free to dress however you like. You're the boss.'

'New shirt?' He pretended to give it his full attention. 'Nice colour, although the summer gear's going to have to go into hibernation pretty soon. Still, very pretty. Preferred the green one, though.' It amused him that she handled his sense of humour by ignoring him. He wasn't used to being ignored, and it was beginning to cross his mind that when it came to women a change could be as good as a rest. Her attitude was certainly welcome relief from the daily, breathless phone-calls he got from Amanda and her constant complaints that he needed to make more time for her.

'How was James this morning?'

'Great.' She looked up and smiled. 'He's walking more and

more without his stick, and he's mentioned having a swimming-pool installed. An indoors one, nothing big. But he said that he still has a lot of contacts in the contracting world and he doesn't think there would be a problem. He's been told by his consultant that swimming would be excellent exercise, and he refuses to think about using the public baths because he says they're full of unidentifiable bacteria. I think he included all kids in that category. What do you think?'

Andreas pushed himself away from his desk and leaned back in his chair. 'I'll have a chat with him later. Can't see there would be any problem aside from the temporary chaos.'

'How did your conference call go last night?' She had been brought up to speed about most of his large clients at dizzying speed. He expected her to know what and whom he was talking about, and to access information without discernible markers.

'Good. Successful. Tiring.' He leant forward and rubbed his thumbs against his eyes.

'You look exhausted,' she ventured, because this was the first time she had seen him succumb to something as pedestrian as tiredness. 'What time did you stay up on that call? It's really important to get sufficient sleep, you know.'

'You're nagging,' Andreas said irritably. 'Women who nag get on my nerves.' He could feel the dull pain of a headache on the rise, and correspondingly he glowered at Elizabeth. Feeling even slightly under the weather was alien to him. He had always embraced robust good health.

'I can't imagine that there would be any woman brave enough to do that,' Elizabeth said calmly.

'*You* just did.'

'I wasn't nagging. I was just stating a fact. If you want to run yourself into the ground, then go ahead.'

'Since when did you get so mouthy?'

Elizabeth decided that silence might be the most prudent

response. Provocative he might sometimes be, but it was unlike him to pick an argument. She was uneasily aware that, were she to be on the receiving end of an argument with Andreas, she would be the loser. She also knew that, although he had stopped referring to her 'hidden agenda' and the need to watch her like a hawk, he was her boss for a reason.

With an impatient scowl, he swung away from her unresponsive, down-bent head and moved straight into a series of instructions which would have defeated all but the highly trained.

She was a damned good secretary. She might have downplayed her ability to go to university and study law, but it was as plain as the nose on his face that the woman was not without brains. She also learnt fast, and her role as secretary, which he'd thought would have been a fiasco of shredded nerves and blushing awkwardness, had somehow transformed her into a finely tuned, efficient working-machine.

It had certainly made the whole business of working from the house a successful venture. Several times he had been obliged to return to London, and on those trips he had used the company helicopter. But, really, operations were running more smoothly than he could ever have imagined possible.

The only problem was that the cool, competent woman was getting on his nerves today.

His headache was also getting worse and that didn't help matters. By the time they finally surfaced from the demands of going over reports, editing documents and analysing data, he could have lain back in the chair and slept.

'Are you all right?'

Andreas grunted at the concerned expression on her face.

'Of course I'm all right!' he snapped. 'Believe it or not, I've never had a day's ill health in my life.'

'Lucky you.'

'What does luck have to do with anything?'

'If that's all for today, Andreas, I think I'll head upstairs now. I promised James a game of chess before dinner.'

'What a thrilling way to spend an evening.' His mobile buzzed and he picked it up, realised that it was Amanda and immediately disconnected. She'd become a nuisance, after he had broken up with her a few days ago, but he was not cad enough to break off all contact entirely. At any rate, he had neither the time nor the inclination to deal with her at the moment.

He looked at Elizabeth who was diligently tidying her desk, obviously eager to be out and away. Chess—at six-thirty on a Friday evening? Was this woman from the same planet as everyone else?

'I enjoy playing chess,' she said, getting into his head and answering his question, which he found a little unsettling. 'I'm not very good but James is a very patient teacher.'

He was scowling, and she felt the hairs on the back of her neck stand on end because she couldn't gauge his mood. Andreas might be a law unto himself but he was very predictable in some areas. He worked hard, and she imagined he played equally hard, although perhaps less so at the moment thanks to the physical constraints of his situation. He expected very high standards in other people because he imposed very high standards on himself. While she continued to resent his fundamental distrust of her, she could acknowledge that he was a fair player. Of course, she had no idea what he was like with the women he dated; he certainly seemed to change them with alarming regularity if James's caustic asides were anything to go by, but that was not her concern.

'Bit dreary, don't you think? Considering your age? Granted, you seem to have lived an abnormally sheltered life, but surely chess on a Friday evening is taking dreary to the outer limits?'

'I'm not into clubs,' Elizabeth muttered, hovering by the door.

'Spot of luck there, then. Not too many of those in the village. There are men, though…or are you not into them either?' Her change of clothes had done wonders for her figure. In fact, he daily appreciated the tantalising sight of cleavage and legs, both of which had been firmly under wraps before.

'I don't think I have to answer that.' Her cheeks were burning; the protective shield of her working gear no longer seemed to be keeping their part of the bargain. Just like that he could strip away her fragile composure, and he did it for no better reason than because he could. 'You forced me to work as your secretary, and I'm doing it, but working as your secretary doesn't mean that I have to answer lots of personal questions.'

'I'm not asking you *lots of personal questions*. I'm showing interest and concern here. James would be upset if you walked away because you were bored with your surroundings.'

'Well, I'm not, and there's no chance of that.'

'Do you know?' Andreas drawled, pushing his chair away from the desk and then stretching out his long legs at an angle. 'It never once occurred to me that you might not have targeted James as a potential sugar-daddy…'

'I know—and what's the point in talking about it if you don't believe what I say?'

'But there could be another explanation for your mysterious arrival in Somerset.' He had mocked her for wanting to spend her Friday cooped up in front of a chessboard, but the truth was that his own plans for heading back to London for the weekend did not appeal. His headache was gathering force and the prospect of having to endure Amanda and her predictable sulks because he had cancelled their last date, due to work, was a turn off. Maybe he would join them at the chess board. Wouldn't that put a spoke in her wheel?

'Am I supposed to ask you what you're talking about?'

'Four weeks ago, you would never have dreamt of saying something like that—I approve! And there's no need to ask me anything, since I'll fill in the gaps for you. You might not have been running *here* so much as *running away.*'

'Running away from what?'

'Or...whom? Is that why you're so happy to bury yourself down here? Because you're recovering from a broken heart?'

'I'm recovering from my mum's death. When I was looking after her, I had little enough time for myself, never mind getting involved with someone!'

'What about that ex-boss of yours? It's easy to fall for someone who's around all the time.'

'Well, I *didn't,* and none of this is any of your business anyway!'

'True. But I thought it might be nice to get to know one another.'

'I think I know you perfectly well enough, thank you very much,' Elizabeth informed him, *sotto voce* so that he couldn't quite grasp what she had said—although he knew from the mutinous expression on her face that it was nothing to his credit.

Well, at least this verbal fencing was taking his mind off his throbbing head, something that the piles of work had not quite managed to do.

'I take my personal assistant out once a month. It's a chance for her to air whatever problems she might have and to recognise that she's appreciated.'

'That's a normal boss-secretary situation, though, isn't it? You haven't forced her to work for you *or else.*'

'Don't tell me that you don't enjoy what you're doing, Elizabeth. You get a buzz working for me, whether you're big enough to admit it or not.'

'I don't get a buzz thinking that you're watching my every move waiting to see if I'll crash and burn.'

'Which isn't much of an answer.'

'This is silly. I'm going to head upstairs now and get changed for the evening. I'll make sure that I do those reports for you so that you have them first thing on Monday morning. In fact, you can have them by tomorrow evening, but I expect you'll be going back to London for the weekend.' *Because you haven't taken dreary to the outer limits,* she found herself thinking sourly.

Andreas stood up, and the ache in his head that had been nudging him insistently for the past hour and a half exploded like a hand grenade suddenly detonated. He braced himself against his desk.

For a few seconds, the only thing Elizabeth felt was blind panic. She was at his side before he could fully recover, although when she anxiously asked him what was wrong he typically waved her aside and bit out that he was perfectly all right.

'No, you're not. You're white as a sheet. You need to get to bed.'

'You need to stop fussing.'

'Shut up.'

Andreas looked so shocked that she was tempted to laugh. Instead, she slung her arm around his waist to help support him.

'What the hell do you think you're doing?'

'Taking you up to bed.' The weight of his arm around her shoulders carried the heat of a branding iron. Never before had she felt so conscious of her own unremarkable body. Her breasts were only inches away from his heavy arm, and her nipples tingled at the proximity so that she had to grit her teeth and focus her mind on the laborious task of helping him up the stairs—when he clearly didn't want any help, and certainly not from her. Although he needed it, judging from his pained breathing and the glazed look in his eyes.

'I. Am. Fine.'

'You seem to have a fever.'

'That's impossible. Like I told you before, I'm never ill.'

'Have you tried telling that to your body?'

'Okay, maybe I could use a few minutes' peace and quiet in the bedroom.'

'What time did you say you got to bed last night?'

Miraculously, and without him really noticing, they appeared to have made it to the top of the stairs. While her support was pretty non-essential, it still felt good to be shown to his room and to watch as she folded back his covers, her movements neat, precise and graceful.

'Haven't I heard the sermon about early nights already?' His hands felt shaky as he began tugging off his shirt. Elizabeth, with her back to him, was only aware of this strip-tease when she heard the sound of his belt being pulled through its loops, and she spun round, her eyes wide.

'You're…getting undressed.'

'I prefer to do that before I get into bed. It really works for me, not getting under the quilt with my trousers and shoes still on.' He felt shattered now that the sight of a welcoming bed was in front of him. He reached to his trouser zip, hardly noticing that she had shied away towards the door.

'I'll…I'll pop up with some paracetamol,' Elizabeth babbled, torn between the need to avert her eyes from those trousers slowly dropping to the ground and the mesmerising sight of his long, muscular legs, the low-slung boxers and the lean, sinewy lines of his torso.

'Thanks.'

He turned around briefly and she hurriedly put her eyes where they should have been—on his face—concerned but in a professional way, the concern of an employee towards her boss.

He was slipping under the covers as she scrambled down the stairs, delayed by James, whose mouth sagged open in astonishment when told that his godson was upstairs. In bed. At the ridiculous time of six-fifteen. Ill.

'The boy's never ill!' he boomed. 'Must be serious. Call the doctor! Number's in that console thing in the kitchen, second drawer down. Name's Stevens, and don't give him a choice about whether he comes out for a house call or not. On second thoughts, *I'll* make the call. Might have to remind him that his surgery got built in double-quick time thanks to my input. Never hurts to call in a favour!'

They had been walking to the kitchen, and while Elizabeth filled a glass with water and hunted down the tablets James telephoned the doctor and managed to turn a simple case of overwork combined with a virus of sorts into a medical emergency.

Andreas wasn't going to be impressed with the fuss, she thought. He wasn't the sort who enjoyed being vulnerable and he was so convinced of his own physical invincibility that she half-expected to find him out of the bed and fully dressed to return to his work.

He wasn't. In fact, he barely spared her a glance as she placed the tablets and water on the table next to his bed, just waving her away and rolling onto his side.

'You should at least take these.' Elizabeth tapped him on his shoulder and he rolled back to face her, dislodging the covers as he heaved his big body up.

'Okay, Ms Nightingale.'

'It's for your own good,' Elizabeth said stiffly. 'I know you think you're invincible, but you're not, and these will help you to feel better.' She watched the ripple of his muscles as he raised the glass to his lips and swallowed back both tablets at once. 'And I think I ought to warn you that James insisted on calling the doctor, even though I told him that there's nothing wrong with you.'

'How do you know that there's nothing wrong with me? Are you a qualified doctor?'

'Well, no, but…'

'I feel terrible.'

'Yes, but it's probably just a combination of too much work, too little sleep and a bit of a bug.'

Andreas gave a snort of scepticism at her diagnosis. 'I think what I have is more than just a *bit of a bug.*' He looked at her fidgeting by the door and frowned. 'I'm burning up. You said so yourself.'

'The tablets should take care of that.'

'You'd better bring me my laptop. No, scratch that. For once I don't feel up to reading reports.' He lay back and closed his eyes while Elizabeth wondered whether this was her form of dismissal. 'I think I need something to eat,' he told her just as she was about to slip quietly away. 'Nothing too heavy. And bring me my mobile. I need to make a few calls to cancel arrangements for the weekend. There's no way I intend to head up to London when I'm at death's door.'

Elizabeth's mouth twitched but she stifled her insane desire to giggle sufficiently to ask him what sort of not-too-heavy meal he had in mind.

'Use your imagination, Florence Nightingale. And you'd better tell James to stay well away in case what I've got is infectious.'

'So it's okay if I catch it?'

'You've spent the afternoon closeted in a room with me. If you're going to catch it, then you already have, and anyway that's a good thing. Means you can transfer operations to the bedroom if you have to.'

'You're kidding, right?'

'Of course I'm kidding,' Andreas said irritably. 'Now, run along. I'm going to grab a few minutes' sleep.'

This time, she recognised the signs of dismissal—namely the fact that she was faced with his broad, bronzed back and all signs of a man settling down for some shut-eye.

'He's being very dramatic,' she grumbled to James, having made a hurried trip back up to the bedroom so that she could deliver his mobile phone, and then having spent half an hour making several calls to clients with whom social meetings had been arranged for the weekend. Scrambled eggs had been requested and had been put on hold while a frazzled doctor disappeared upstairs to conduct what she personally thought would be a pointless examination.

'He's never ill.' James was comfortable in his favourite padded chair by the bay window of the small snug off the kitchen.

'I'm not surprised,' Elizabeth said tartly. 'What germs would have the temerity to set up camp near him?'

'Your colour's all up.' James's blue eyes were shrewd as he took in her flushed face. 'Hope you're not about to pick up whatever damn fool bug he's got. Go have yourself a bath, woman. Get changed into your comfy clothes. Can't imagine what possessed you to start wearing fancy gear just because you're taking a few notes for that godson of mine!'

'It's not *fancy gear,*' she said awkwardly. 'But, yes, I'll go change. I'll make it quick.' She spontaneously dropped a kiss on the old man's cheek, and he huffed and puffed to conceal his thrill at that passing gesture of affection.

'And don't forget that game of chess!' he barked to her departing back. 'Though I'll quite understand if you want to put an old fool like me on hold in favour of a good-looking man upstairs. Don't go thinking that I don't know my place in life!'

If only James knew, she thought as she very quickly showered and changed into a pair of jeans and a long-sleeved cotton top, just how secure his place in her life was. So secure that she had begun thinking that maybe she would never admit her real identity to him. Would it be such a sin to do everything within her power to avoid jeopardising what she had—a wonderful relationship with a man who only months ago she had not even known existed? Where would be the harm in just quietly destroying those incriminating letters? In no longer having to live with the fear of wondering how James would react to revelations that could destroy his faith in her and rock the foundations of his fragile existence.

She put aside the nagging questions as she hurried downstairs just in time to catch the doctor's final words, that Andreas was suffering from little more than a bad bout of the end-of-summer cold that was doing its rounds through the country.

'There,' she told James. 'Didn't I tell you? Nothing at all to worry about.' This she said as she poured three beaten eggs into a frying pan and stuck a couple of pieces of bread into the toaster.

'*You* seem to be the one pandering to his needs,' James pointed out with his usual lack of diplomacy.

'Just obeying orders,' Elizabeth informed him loftily. 'The Great One wanted something to eat.'

'Go tell him that your secretarial duties are done for the day! Maria can take the food up.'

'Well, it's done now.' She shrugged while an uneasy voice in her head told her that she *wanted* to take the food up to Andreas. 'Besides, Maria will be busy, you know? Getting your supper ready.'

She refused to look at James as she piled the food onto a tray, but she was keenly aware of his penetrating blue gaze on her. She exited the kitchen to exuberant exclamations about perhaps adding a flower in a vase to the picture-perfect tray in her hands.

Thoroughly disgruntled, her first words as she entered the

bedroom were, 'Apparently you're not at death's door,' followed quickly by, 'Why on earth are the curtains drawn? It's like a morgue in here!'

She walked across to the curtains and pulled them open, allowing the weak light to stream through. The brilliant weather had culminated in the usual British summer of hazy sunshine interspersed with plentiful supplies of rain. Through the windows, she could see the lawns had not quite managed to shrug off the day's earlier downpour, the grass glistened down below.

'Where is that softly spoken, blushing, awkward girl who used to work here?' Andreas squinted at the invading light. 'When did she get replaced by a nagging harridan?'

'I've brought you something to eat. As ordered.'

'Requested,' Andreas amended, watching as she went to fetch the tray which she had set down on the chest-of-drawers. He didn't have to look at her at all. Not really. Somehow, the shape of her had become imprinted on his mind. Her breasts were big for someone who wasn't very tall. In fact, bigger than Amanda's, who had a good six inches over Elizabeth in height. Her eyes were luminous green, and refreshingly she didn't bat them at him in a girlish attempt to get herself noticed. And that hair…always tied up and clipped into order, but rebellious tendrils held the promise of luxuriant abundance. He wondered what it would feel like to yank out those pins, clips and grips and curl his fingers into its burnished, coppery thickness.

He pushed himself into a sitting position so that she could place the tray on his lap, but when she would have left the room he patted a space next to him, although he wasn't looking at her as he dug his fork into the egg,

'I'm not well,' he said piously. 'I really could do with the company.'

'You have a cold.' She eyed the vacant spot his hand had signalled and gingerly perched at the very edge of the mattress. 'I don't think it's anything to get too worried about.'

'More than just a *cold,*' Andreas corrected.

'But, thank goodness, your appetite's not affected.'

'It's important to build up my immune system.' He glanced at her with lazy interest. 'You surprise me. I thought you might have been a little more sympathetic. You're a self-proclaimed carer, after all.'

'And *I* thought that the last person on the face of the earth who would succumb to feeling sorry for himself over a cold would be *you!*' Being this close to him was making her feel jittery. The way he was looking at her was making her feel jittery as well; his dark eyes shuttered and brooding as he made short work of the food she had placed in front of him. 'I guess, since your motto is "why put in one-hundred percent when you can put in one hundred and ten?" you maybe feel that you have to be extreme even when you're a bit under the weather. You'll just be *more* under the weather than anybody else!'

Andreas gave it some thought. 'You know me better than I know myself,' he murmured, and she reddened, immediately lost for words. In truth the tablets had kicked in, but now that he was in bed, being brought food like an invalid, he was enjoying the sensation of just taking time out to stand still. When was the last time his brain hadn't been on the move? When was the last time he hadn't been firing on all cylinders at a pace that left everybody else trailing behind? The doctor had told him that his lifestyle had opened him up to a virus, that often times it was only when a person slowed down that the weight of constant stress and constant activity finally caught up. Working down in Somerset had been that slowing down, and, hell, it felt good not to be doing anything at all.

He would never live it down with his godfather, who had

always made it a habit to lecture him on his frenetic lifestyle. So, naturally, he would keep the doctor's pearls of wisdom to himself.

And in the meantime….

'Maybe you're right. I'm not equipped to deal with illness.'

'At least not unless you're hamming it up and behaving like a drama queen,' she couldn't resist qualifying. 'Now, I think I ought to leave you to get some sleep.'

'I don't need sleep. In fact, it's the last thing I need. I should really catch up on some emails.'

'Work is the last thing you should be thinking about—as you're bed-ridden.' She couldn't stop herself from smirking at his overblown response to a light fever and headache, although there was something stupidly endearing about it all the same.

'You're right,' Andreas agreed with alacrity. 'You're going to fall off the bed if you get any closer to the side. Don't worry—I won't bite.' He paused to consider that rider and gave a wolfish smile that sent a little tingling shiver through her. His keen eyes took in that automatic response, indicating an awareness to which she would never admit. From being nervous and on edge around him, she had slotted into her role of secretary, and her efficiency, her composure when involved in work, was so ingrained that a great deal of her edginess had been pushed into the background. Only at times like these, when she couldn't call upon that ingrained composure to protect her, was he keenly aware of her awkward, very girlish and excessively feminine responses.

Sure, he had got no closer to finding out what had brought her down to Somerset, or even whether the scant information gleaned from her ex-boss was even relevant. Naturally he still cared, because rich men were natural targets for unscrupulous women, but at what point did he just hold his hands up in defeat and let her get on with whatever she had planned—if anything? He would have to put a deadline on his stay in Somerset, despite what he had said about remaining here for the foreseeable future. Strangely, the allure of London, with its cut-throat pace, was failing to weave its magic spell. Give it another month and he'd be chewing on a twig, adopting a West Country burr and *still* would probably be nowhere near finding out what the hell she was up to.

He was reluctantly beginning to acknowledge the fact that a man never knew what the hell was going on in a woman's mind. How could someone be transparent and opaque at the same time? Be practical yet ditzy? Composed under pressure but addled in the most relaxed surroundings—like now? Lazy, predatorial eyes took in everything about her, from the tension that had her sitting upright like a wooden marionette, to the very slight tremble of her fingers and the beating pulse just there at the side of her neck.

He was sick of waiting for her to slip up and reveal something, anything, that could put his mind at rest, that could reassure him she could be fully trusted.

There had to be better and more interesting ways to get information—and his whirring, inventive brain was already beginning to come up with one.

CHAPTER FIVE

ELIZABETH was having a dream. In the dream, a high, terrifying wind was raging outside and the branches of the trees were tapping hard against the window panes like scrawny fingers trying to grab her attention. But her attention was somewhere else. It was on the man in the bed with her. His bronzed, muscular limbs were wrapped around her so that their bodies were a tangle of light and dark. His hands were curled into her hair, which was strewn across the pillow, and she was writhing and moaning as he touched every part of her, from her face down to her toes. Even in the dream there was still a part of her that found it difficult to equate the sensuous, uninhibited creature with the person she knew she was.

She came to very slowly to the sound of someone rapping on her bedroom door, and when she groggily sat up the little pink alarm-clock at the side of her bed informed her that it was three in the morning.

It took a few seconds for her to disentangle herself from the debauched eroticism of her dream, and a few more seconds for her to appreciate that rapping on her door at a ridiculous hour could only herald bad news—which could only mean that there was something wrong with James, even though he had been as fit as a fiddle when she had said goodnight to him six hours previously. Having lived with the vagaries of her mother's health for two years, she was well aware how quickly a downturn could happen.

She flung on her dressing gown and was fumbling with the sash as she pulled open the door.

Having mentally braced herself to see James, and having halfway worked out a worst-case scenario and how she would deal with it, she was poleaxed to discover that her late-night caller was Andreas. He was in a bathrobe, which was thick and black; since he hadn't bothered to do anything as mundane as belt it, it was hanging open, revealing boxer shorts and nothing else.

Still hot and bothered from the sexy, abandoned, graphic nature of her dream, she was excruciatingly aware of his black eyes boring through her skull, and said a quick prayer of thanks that he actually couldn't drag her wicked thoughts out of her head by sheer will-power.

'What do you want?'

'I've just spent the last twenty minutes foraging for some more tablets downstairs. Where in God's name do you keep them?'

'You woke me up at *three in the morning* because you need some *paracetomol?*'

'I'm ill. Too ill to spend the rest of what remains of my valuable down-time hunting through kitchen drawers.' Rumpled from sleep, Elizabeth's eyes were drowsy, and her hair hung down her back in a tangle of copper curls. Gone was the super-efficient secretary; gone was the bumbling, gauche girl who had planted terrified green eyes on him the first time he had seen her. In her place was a small, sexy Elizabeth, one who was definitely *all woman.* She tightly belted her dressing gown with a fierce little tug and made an indeterminate, disgruntled sound under her breath.

'This is ridiculous,' she muttered, sweeping past him and feeling the brush of his skin against hers with red-hot, electric sensitivity. 'Didn't you think to take the pack up with you, along with a glass of water?'

'I'm not accustomed to the routines of sick people.'

'It's not a *routine.* It's common sense.' She could feel his eyes on her as she descended the staircase in darkness, moving slowly while her eyes got used to the lack of light, then switching on the lamp on the table at the bottom of the stairs. She spun round to shoot him an accusing look—a look that said 'this is definitely not one of my expected secretarial duties'—and discovered that he was so close behind her that their bodies were almost touching.

Expert as Andreas was in the shades and nuances of female behaviour, he noted the way she shifted back in alarm. She could no longer hide behind her neat, prissy, secretarial uniform, and that would be bothering her. He would bet his enormous fortune on her tightening the strangulating belt around her waist with another decisive tug, and sure enough she did.

Elizabeth turned away, walking briskly towards the kitchen, and then beyond the kitchen to the larder. She pulled the little step-ladder from the corner, flipped it open and stepped on it so that she could reach the top shelf, where all the medicines were kept in two sealed, plastic containers.

'I don't suppose you thought to look here?' she said tartly, turning round to find that she was looking down at him. Only a little bit, but it was a first.

'Would I have woken you if I had?'

'I don't know. You certainly seem to be making the most out of a passing summer cold.'

Andreas didn't answer. Instead he reached forward and Elizabeth felt his big hands wrap around her slender torso. Then she was pulled from the step-ladder, spluttering and red-faced.

'What do you think you're doing?'

He deposited her on the ground and she leapt back to glare at him. 'I'm being solicitous. I thought you might have appreciated the gesture.'

Elizabeth tried to dust herself off, from where her skin literally burnt from being touched, while Andreas looked on with amusement. He didn't look ill. A bit flushed in the face, maybe, but not as much as she was at the moment after that ridiculous, unnecessary act of so-called chivalry. In the time that she had been working for him, not once had he laid a finger on her!

Except, she wasn't wearing her secretarial hat now, was she? She was wearing a dressing gown and not much else underneath. A dressing gown that had loosened when he had hauled her off her step-ladder, where she had been feeling quite comfortable staring down at him instead of the other way around. She made a nervous little movement to straighten herself, and thrust the box of tablets into his hand.

'I take it you know where the water is? And glasses?'

'Either I make you nervous…' Andreas lazily rolled the box of tablets between his long fingers while he looked at her with slumberous dark eyes '…and you become twitchy and flustered, or else I make you nervous and you go for my jugular.'

'You *don't* make me nervous!' For the first time, there was a comforting ring of truth about this. Gone was the time when the mere knowledge that he was occupying the same space as her was enough to turn her insides to water, much like a rabbit stuck in the same room as a python. No, he didn't make her nervous in *that* way any more. She had become accustomed to him, and could handle the ferocity of his intelligence and his unpredictability with a lot more composure now. It was a useful thought, and one in which she decided to take immediate comfort. 'And I'm not going for *your jugular.*' She wished he would get out of her way because he was standing in front of the door to the larder, blocking her in, but she quailed at the thought of trying to push past him.

She folded her arms decisively and gave him a beetling look, which was a mistake, because instead of putting a stop to their silly conversation it brought a slow, curling smile to his sensuous mouth.

'I'm glad I no longer make you nervous,' Andreas said huskily. 'It shows that we're getting to know one another, getting more comfortable in each other's company. Wouldn't you agree?' He leaned against the doorframe in the manner of one settling in for the long haul.

'I've become accustomed to your mood swings, I suppose.'

'Mood swings? I don't consider myself a moody person.'

'There are several people who have been on the receiving end of your conversations who might be inclined to disagree. Anyway, Andreas, it's late.' She produced a yawn, which developed into a real one, and ran her fingers through her unrestrained hair. More than anything else, she felt that her over-long hair, which was unruly and uncontrollable and which should have been cut a long time ago, put her at a disadvantage. It made her too aware of her own female sexuality in a way that was unwelcome and discomforting. It was bad enough working alongside the man, having to make sure that she could take refuge behind her strict working-clothes and working persona, without having to face him without her work hat in place.

'If you don't mind…?' She looked significantly at the door which he continued to block, and Andreas meekly stood aside with an apologetic expression.

'Of course.'

'I hope you feel better in the morning but, if you don't, just let me know. There are a million and one things that need doing in the village, or else I could spend the afternoon working without you if you think I might be taking advantage otherwise.'

This wasn't what Andreas wanted. He didn't feel nearly as rough as he had implied, and he had been enjoying their little *tête à tête.* In fact, he had been enjoying the confined space of the larder, and the tantalising sight of her wiggling up the little ladder, providing him with a wonderful view of her sexy little derrière, one which he realised he had been covertly looking at ever since he had found himself in close quarters with her in his makeshift office.

What else had he been looking at without even realising? He certainly had been fantasising about seeing that hair in all its glory, and he wasn't disappointed. Indeed, his fingers itched to coil into the long strands so that he could exert control over her stubborn mouth, bring it to meet his and kiss it into begging submission.

He felt his erection stiffen under the bathrobe, kick starting all his natural hunting instincts.

Since when, he wondered, had she begun getting under his skin like this? The tantalising notion of seducing her as a means to an end…who was he kidding? Sure, he still wanted to get inside her head and find out whatever dark little secret she was hiding—but much more than that he just wanted to get into her knickers and explore one or two other places. He wanted to hear her cry out his name and he wanted those feline green eyes, the colour of rain-washed sea, to look at him in the kind of needy, greedy way he would normally discourage in a woman.

In fact, the list of things he wanted to do with her was getting longer by the second.

While she continued to head for the door in the firm manner of a matron bidding a relieved goodnight to a troublesome patient.

'Hey! Just a minute!'

Elizabeth turned around to watch as he casually stuck a glass under the tap, and then turned the tap on to full force so that the water splashed indiscriminately over every nearby surface. Andreas didn't seem bothered. He kept his eyes focused on her as he swallowed the tablets and then dumped the glass on the draining board.

This was just one of the little things she had managed to absorb about him over time. For a bachelor, he was stupendously undomesticated. Mugs were left to form damaging circles on expensive tables; feet were rested on the desk with complete disregard to the fact that, whether or not the shoes on said feet were of exorbitant, hand-made Italian leather, they were still shoes with traces of grime, mud and gravel underneath. On occasion, she had entered the office, punctual to the last minute, to find him absorbed in some item of work with a sandwich in his hand and a riot of crumbs covering most of the exposed surfaces, marking a trail where he had prowled through the room, eating, reading and probably barking out orders to someone on speaker-phone.

'What is it?'

'Aren't you going to escort the patient back to his bed? Make sure he doesn't keel over halfway up the stairs?'

'You're not a *patient. I'm* not a doctor.'

'No, you're my secretary.'

'And is that supposed to mean that this is one of my secretarial duties?'

Andreas's beautiful face tightened into lines of icy derision, and Elizabeth immediately felt contrite. She had thrown his banter back in his face, and established those boundary lines that had been evading her, but she didn't feel victorious. She felt mean, petty and mealy-mouthed. Soiled, even, like someone who only did a good deed in the expectation of being rewarded. Like someone with a bone-deep sense-of-humour failure, incapable of being light-hearted, and quick to reject any show of harmless, innocent teasing.

'I'm sorry. I'm just tired…' She cast her eyes miserably downwards.

'I could always pay you extra—for the extra duties,' Andreas told her with cold reproval. He wasn't ready to let go of his anger because her recoil at the thought of actually accompanying him *up the stairs* had carried the sour taste of rejection, and rejection wasn't a feeling he had ever had much to do with. For the first time, it occurred to him that she had only relaxed in his company over the past few weeks because she had had no choice. She would never have been able to function had she been as tightly stretched as violin wire, and function she had had to do, so she had taken a deep breath and suffered him. Was it possible that the woman genuinely couldn't stand his guts?

The notion flashed through his head and disappeared before it could take root, snuffed out by his inborn self-assurance. But, whatever, watching her eyes widen in alarm at the thought of walking up a dozen stairs in his company still enraged him.

Perversely, his anger did nothing to dissipate the powerful surge of his physical response to her. In fact, the thought of her breathing his name in the throes of passion, begging him to take her, was even more seductive now.

'You're tired,' he said brusquely, walking towards her. 'And I was a fool to have said what I just said. I apologise.'

'Sorry?'

'I apologise,' Andreas told her simply, with a shrug of his broad shoulders. 'And I apologise for waking you for no better reason than to ask where the painkillers were kept.'

'But you're not programmed to think about painkillers.' She allowed herself to smile, glad that that horrible moment of indescribable tension was over. 'Or the practicalities of where to find them when you need them. As you said, you're not accustomed to the routines of a sick person.'

She switched off the kitchen light behind them as they silently headed across the sprawling flag-stoned hallway towards the majestic staircase.

'Do you know,' Elizabeth said softly, tempted into confidence by her curious lightheadedness because they were okay with one another again, 'not a day goes by that I don't appreciate what a glorious house this is?'

'Not to mention a change from a bedsit.' But he was in no mood to introduce a jarring note to their conversation, so he found himself swerving off into that taboo area labelled 'personal' in his head—the door which was usually closed to prying female eyes. 'But I agree with you.'

'You do? Surely you must have become accustomed to all of this over the years?' She heard the wistfulness creep into her voice and cleared her throat.

'I grew up in this house,' Andreas said slowly. 'These grounds were my own private playground. But my father was just an employee here. I don't suppose you knew that.'

Elizabeth shook her head in the darkness and tried to walk as slowly as possible, because Andreas saying anything of a personal nature to her was a moment to be drawn out for as long as humanly possible. She was surprised she was managing to breathe at all.

'No. I didn't.'

'So I may not have lived in a two-up, two-down, but believe me in my head I was always aware that that should have been my fate.' Andreas laughed, vaguely disconcerted that he was doing this whole confiding thing, which he had always presumed to be the exclusive realm of women and one in which he had little interest.

'Didn't—didn't James's wife object to—you know?—having you as a surrogate son, so to speak?' James was never unkind about the woman who had shared his life; as for her mother, the woman who had shared his bed and his heart, she had not once been mentioned. In fact, he seldom mentioned his deceased wife.

'Portia was only interested in herself and in the things James could provide for her materially. She made an excellent hostess, but lord only knows whether the marriage would have lasted beyond the first few years if the money hadn't kept rolling in. So, no, she never objected to myself or my parents. But she made it known that, whilst her husband might like playing the philanthropist, she still saw us as the hired help.' His mouth twisted at the remembered slight, delivered when he'd been barely a teenager. '"Pet projects", she once informed me.' They were at his bedroom door and he realised that he was perspiring slightly—either from his unexpected trip down memory lane, or from the slight fever which was threading through him, despite his valiant efforts to shake it off.

'That's awful.'

'That's life,' Andreas said briefly. 'Still tired, or do you want to turn back the bed and make the invalid happy?' He switched on the bedside lamp and the little circle of mellow light threw him into shadowy relief.

Elizabeth's heart was banging. The atmosphere between them suddenly felt charged, pregnant and heavy with something unspoken, something she couldn't quantify or put her finger on.

'Now I'm a nurse!' She laughed shakily and waited with her back to him, because she really didn't want to see him brush past her to the bed.

'In a manner of speaking, you are. James might be recovering nicely now, but you have had to cater to his physical needs in terms of settling him at night, making sure he takes his daily exercise… Has it occurred to you that the time is coming when he might no longer need you around?'

Elizabeth spun round on her heels and looked at him in open dismay. Yes, that thought had occurred to her, but really only vaguely. Like the increasingly uncomfortable matter of her real identity, she had been content to lay it to one side.

'Has he said that to you?' she asked, fighting to control the tremor in her voice.

Andreas could sense the panic and felt that frustrated surge of curiosity and the accompanying, raging need to find out what lay behind it.

He saw the way her full mouth quivered, and without thinking he reached out and feathered his finger across her lips.

For a split second everything emptied out of her head and even her breathing was arrested. She touched her lips with the tip of her fingers, shocked and surprised to find that they weren't burning hot, which was how they felt. Which was how her entire body felt. The excitement unleashed in her was wild and suffocating. She felt as though she was caught up in the eye of a hurricane, and it took a little while for her brain to crank back into gear and for her to tell herself that the casual gesture meant nothing at all. For a nano-second in time, they had shared their thoughts, and that passing moment had released Andreas's hitherto-unseen ability to sympathise. The guy was human, after all; despite his coldness, his arrogance, his offputting brilliance, there had had to be a few sympathetic genes there somewhere. Incredibly they had found their way to the surface and, sensing her distress, he had offered her a gesture of compassion.

She backed away. Not because she was running scared at the turmoil bubbling up inside her—oh no, she told herself. She was backing away because she really *was* tired, and he really *did* need to get some sleep because it was the best cure for a cold.

'Would you believe, I can feel those tablets kicking in already?'

'Really? Well. That's brilliant.' She was almost at the door thanks to a series of crablike movements that had safely taken her out of his reach. 'A good night's sleep is probably all you need and you'll be fighting fit in the morning.'

'Is that your expert medical opinion?' Andreas smiled drily. 'You have a practical approach when it comes to dealing with ailing men. I'm beginning to see what makes you so good at what you do. You don't humour them and you chivvy.'

'I don't like the word *chivvy.* It sounds too much like *nag.*' She swallowed hard. From across the room, she felt as though he was reaching out and touching her and it sent a strange, icy, exciting chill up and down her spine.

'You don't look like a nag,' Andreas murmured softly.

Like an idiot, Elizabeth heard herself reply on a nervous whisper, 'What do I look like?'

If she wanted to leave, there was nothing stopping her. In fact, she couldn't get nearer to the door if she tried, and although her brain was shrieking at her to run like a bat out of hell her body was saying something else. That something else was keeping her rooted to the spot. In the space of only a few seconds, Andreas's perceptive mind had grasped all of those essentials and was already working out how best to take advantage of the situation—because take advantage of it he certainly would. He blamed his suffocating, single-minded determination to bed her on a variety of reasons, all of which were firmly to do with curiosity, and didn't trouble himself to look further than that. Curiosity was sufficient impetus, as far as he was concerned, because it was a rare commodity in his life and to be savoured for as long as possible.

'I've been curious to see your hair.' He walked towards the bed, removing his bathrobe *en route* so that he was down to just his boxers. He didn't look at her as he said this. He didn't have to. His imagination could fill in the blanks, and the exercise of filling in those blanks—the blushing cheeks, the soft gasp, that nervous way she had of biting her lip—was a turn-on like no other. 'You always wear it up or dragged back from your face.'

He lay down on the bed with the covers half over him and leaned against the headboard with his arms behind his head. 'I've imagined unpinning it,' he admitted with a casual shrug. 'Imagined it tumbling over your shoulders, much as it is now.' The game of seduction had never involved keeping a safe distance from the intended lover or playing it cool the way he was now—lying in bed like the invalid he most certainly wasn't, and pretending that he didn't want to yank her to him and run his fingers through that mane of untamed copper hair; it was so unlikely on someone as unflamboyant as her. At least, on the outside. Which made him wonder how flamboyant she was on the inside. How wild. As wild as her hair? As unrestrained?

Elizabeth's hand self-consciously flew to her hair and then dropped to her side. Her heart was hammering inside her and she could no longer deny to herself that the out-of-body feeling she was having was grounded in the most basic of human responses: lust. Andreas was a gorgeous man, a supreme example of male beauty at its most spectacular. He had the presence and the looks that could stop any woman dead in her tracks; she had not been immune to the raw power of his personality, especially working alongside him.

She had accompanied him down to the kitchen in his hunt for painkillers, even though he really had had a nerve to wake her up in the early hours of the morning for something as silly as that. He would have unearthed the medicine eventually. In fact, she could have just told him where they were, something that only now belatedly occurred to her. But she hadn't, had she? As always when he asked her to do something beyond the call of duty—to work overtime, to fetch him something to eat because he couldn't possibly break away from whatever mega-important thing he happened to be in the middle of doing—she had sighed and grumbled to herself. But did she ever refuse? No. Did she ever seriously consider refusing? No.

She gave herself long lectures about resenting him. She told herself that he was dangerous in his pursuit to discover what he thought she was hiding, and should therefore be handled with caution, like a temperamental Rottweiler. She made long lists in her head about all the hateful things about him. And yet her body was still her own worst enemy.

'Um…it's more convenient to tie it back during the day.' She was astounded that her vocal chords were continuing to function when every other function that required her mind to work seemed hellbent on shutting down.

'I…I should have had it cut ages ago,' she stumbled over her words as he continued to look at her with unnerving intensity. 'But everything's been so chaotic over the past few months—well, longer than that, actually. In fact, I can't even remember when I last had my hair cut.' She had to make a conscious effort not to reach and twist it into a knot, get it out of the way, remove it from being a subject for conversation. 'Ages ago,' she finished lamely.

'I'm glad.'

'You are?'

With the finely tuned predatorial instincts of a shark, Andreas breathed in the tantalising smell of imminent conquest; never before had it smelt so *good.* He smiled. 'It may be my imagination, but women these days have tailored hair. It's unusual to find someone who doesn't fuss about what she looks like.'

'That's not a very kind thing to say.'

'Coming from me, you can take it as the highest compliment. I get sick to death of stick-thin creatures with poker-straight hair and layers of make-up.' Which fitted the description of Amanda down to the letter, but that was no longer his problem, now that he had broken up with her.

It had been a while coming, something he hadn't mentioned when he had arranged to meet her when he had been to London a couple of days previously. Instead, he had listened to her ranting and railing, had politely handed over his handkerchief when she had started crying and had made his excuses and left when she had started implying that they could try and make things work. It had been just the right time to leave, because he had shut the door of her apartment to the sound of her mounting anger, a woman scorned.

He sounded, to Elizabeth, as though he was surprised to have come to that conclusion. On that flattering note of sincerity, Elizabeth knew that she should leave, because she was feeling more giddy by the minute. But when he told her to stop hovering by the door, and patted a space beside him on the bed, she was aware of herself walking towards him in a zombie-like trance.

'So…' Andreas drawled, 'are you going to let me assuage my curiosity?' His arms were still folded behind his head, but beneath the covers the urgency of his erection stirred and stiffened.

The thought of Andreas 'assuaging his curiosity' on her opened up boundless visions in her head that were scary and enticing at the same time. She felt herself break out in fine perspiration. His remark might go against every romantic notion in her head, but there was a raw, animal urgency to it that brought her out in goosebumps.

Elizabeth had never, ever, not even once in passing, been

the object of such blazing, brilliant intensity as she was now. Like some kind of potent drug, it went to her head and zapped out all thoughts of caution. She shifted slightly and her hair fell over one shoulder, its curling tips almost touching the covers loosely draped over Andreas's sexy, bronzed body.

He shot her a slow, curling smile that shattered her already fast-crumbling defence system and made her breath catch in her throat. Her last attempt to focus was a lame, 'You really should get some sleep now…' which trailed off into a suffocating sense of anticipation, sharpening all her senses and making her feel as though time was standing still.

Andreas reached forward and lazily twirled one long strand of hair between his fingers, which he looked at in apparent fascination. Then he pulled her to him. In the process, her dressing gown fell open, and when she automatically reached to preserve her modesty he held her straying hand fast in his.

'Amazingly, I've wanted to do this for a while,' he murmured as his lips touched hers, gentle and exploratory at first, then hungry and insistent as she tumbled onto the bed next to him; he curved his body so that his heavy thigh pinned her down.

Elizabeth clung to him. Shorn of all the arguments she had constructed to distance herself from the magnetic pull he had over her, her craving was an unstoppable force. She emitted a soft whimper as his tongue delved and thrust deeply in her mouth, and she began running her trembling hands over his naked body. Like a blind person acquainting themselves with someone else's body through touch, she traced the contours of his torso and lost herself in the wonder of his hard, densely packed muscle.

'I take it you feel the same way,' Andreas murmured into her mouth. Her nod and accompanying whimper was all he could have hoped for. 'Then touch me,' he whispered hoarsely.

'Feel for yourself exactly how much I've been fantasising about you.' He took her hand in his and directed it to where his erection was as hard as steel, and he groaned as she wrapped her fingers around it and began simulating the rubbing motion he might have experienced during intercourse. He had to press down hard on her hand to stop her, or else he would have done the unthinkable and climaxed before he wanted to, something he had never done in his life before.

'Okay…' His voice was husky and unsteady. 'Let's take this slowly…' He flattened her to the bed and pinned down both her hands with his, then he levered his big body so that he was straddling her but not touching her.

Elizabeth almost fainted at the sight of his magnificent manhood rearing up from its nest of dark curls. His black robe was like a marauding cape, but he got rid of that swiftly, returning his hand to hers and letting her enjoy the sight of his rampant masculinity.

'Don't move a muscle,' he commanded, and she obeyed, her eyes fluttering shut as he undid the sash of her robe and peeled it back to expose her naked breasts.

She was beyond beautiful, way beyond what he had imagined. She still had her hands raised above her head, her fists tightly closed, as were her eyes. Andreas stroked her neck with his fingers, and this time when he kissed her it was long and lingering and an indication that he wasn't going to rush their love-making. As cures for the common summer-cold went, this beat the hell out of a couple of tablets; he had never felt more alive or vibrant.

Taking his time, he let his lips blaze a trail along her collarbone, then down to her breasts. It was agonisingly difficult to ignore those pert, pink nipples pouting at him, but ignore them he did, at least for a few minutes while he attended to her cleavage. Then he turned his attention to those big discs, bigger than average for the size of her breasts, which were generous, more than a handful.

Delicately, he circled his tongue over the stiffened bud and she shuddered convulsively. He had told her to keep her hands where they were, not to move a muscle, but she just couldn't remain like a frozen statue when she wanted more than delicacy. She clasped her fingers in his hair and watched in dazed fascination at her own hands pushing his head down against her breast so that he could take her sensitive, aching nipple into his mouth; so that he could roll his tongue abrasively over its surface until she wanted to scream from the sensation.

A guttural moan escaped her lips as he suckled hard on her, drawing the tip into his mouth and teasing it with his tongue, while the wetness of his mouth started a frenzy of liquid excitement coursing through her veins. He stilled her restive writhing by placing one hand firmly over her feminine mound, still sheathed in its cotton underwear through which she just knew he could feel the dampness that was the glaring evidence of how much she was aroused.

She moved against his hand and angled her body against the ridge of his finger which immediately made him release her so that he could waggle another finger with disapproval, grinning.

'No way,' he murmured. 'When you come, I want to be the one to take you there.' He worked his way further down her body, enjoying the satiny smoothness of her belly, pausing to circle her belly button with his tongue. Then very slowly he divested her of her cotton briefs.

He breathed her in. She smelt dewy and sweet, and he deftly parted her legs so that he could gaze down at the soft fold of skin, from which spilled the wetness of her need as great as his own. He dipped his tongue in between that crease, tasting her honeyed sweetness, and Elizabeth gave a convulsive little shiver and shielded her face with her arm.

She couldn't look at him. If she did, she was convinced that she would teeter over the brink from the mere sight of his dark head between her legs, doing things to her that no one had ever done before, and which she was enjoying beyond belief. Her body was behaving with a will of its own, rising up to meet his mouth as his tongue thrust deeper and harder against her throbbing clitoris.

She badly wanted to feel him inside her, but like a maestro in expert charge of his instrument Andreas knew just when to stop before they *both* came prematurely.

It was a matter of seconds for him to avail himself of the necessary contraception, seconds during which Elizabeth touched herself, because she just had to. Then, with a groan of satisfaction that he barely recognised himself making, he entered her, driving deeply, his big body rearing up as he thrust faster, harder, until he felt her climax against him, and until he too shuddered at his own soul-shattering orgasm.

CHAPTER SIX

'YOU'RE late.' Andreas looked pointedly at his watch as Elizabeth pushed open the door to the office forty-five minutes after she should have been there. Under normal circumstances, this would not have been a problem for him. With ultra-efficiency, she had made sure that everything he needed for his reports—right down to miniscule logistic details that even his more experienced secretary in London would have omitted—were ready before he had switched on his computer at seven in the morning. Which meant that she had emailed him the information way after official closing time. He should not even have noticed her late entry, because in his world closing a deal was always the only thing that mattered.

Unfortunately for him, focusing had proved impossible. In fact, in the week since they had become lovers, she had managed to wreak havoc with his concentration levels, so it could be said that 'normal circumstances' had been put on temporary hold.

She'd point-blank refused to condone any risky behaviour while she was working with him, even though he had assured her that this was definitely one occasion when he would freely mix pleasure with business.

'A desk,' he had told her invitingly, 'would be a hell of a

lot more interesting with you sprawled on top of it, fully dressed except for your knickers. I needn't even leave my chair! You would just need to open your legs and I would be at the perfect height to sample what's on offer between them with my mouth…' She had laughed, blushed and refused, at which point he had attempted to interest her in the sofa by the bookcase or even his large, leather swivel-chair. Both items of furniture had met with the same negative response. Andreas didn't get it.

'I wouldn't dream of issuing an offer like that to anyone else who worked with me. In fact, it's a personal rule of mine never to mix business with pleasure.'

'And it's a brilliant one. Inter-office relationships muddy the waters.'

'Are you speaking from experience?'

'Only as a spectator.'

'I don't think you understand. The fact that I'm willing to make you the exception to my rule should be viewed as the highest compliment.'

It had been viewed with a shake of her head, the slow purr of her computer being switched on and that prim crossing of her legs which did crazy things to his libido.

It was damned frustrating. Was it any wonder that he was constantly distracted? For the first time, his work was taking second place. He didn't like it, but sleeping with her had unearthed a vein of stubbornness that he hadn't noticed in her before. He had had to fall in with her ridiculous rules and regulations about keeping their work-space sacrosanct.

Was it some sort of wily game she was playing? Was she stringing him along because she thought it would be the fastest way of keeping him interested? Was she a cunning gold-digger who had now dropped his godfather off her hit list so that she could focus her attentions on him instead? He couldn't have cared less. His plans to uncover whatever she was or wasn't hiding from him had been derailed and frankly ambushed by a raging, uncontrollable lust that seemed to have become his twenty-four-hour companion.

Now, when she should have been feeling the same way, when she should have been angling to spend every conceivable moment in his company, even if only to experience the frisson of being in the same room as him during their allotted work-time, she strolled in nearly an hour late.

Andreas scowled.

'Sorry.' Elizabeth smiled apologetically as she pulled out her chair and settled into it.

It was getting harder and harder to split herself in two—the wild, abandoned, uninhibited lover late at night when the rest of the world was asleep, and the professional by day, keeping him at arm's length. Ignoring the subtle but invasive ways he had of making his formidable presence known by brushing her arm when he leant over her to explain something, or looking at her with brooding, greedy eyes as she sat there with her notepad on her lap jotting down points, numbers and figures; his mind never seemed to stop working even when his body language was signalling something else.

He wanted her, and he wanted to be able to have her at the click of his imperious fingers. It was a situation Elizabeth knew was dangerous and unhealthy. She was already way out of her depth. Keeping a bit of distance was vital.

But, on the plus side, she had at least made one very important decision that had lessened some of the weight on her shoulders. She had more or less put on permanent hold the notion of telling James who she was. She could see no advantage in it and many, many disadvantages. If James was in the slightest bit protective of his wealth—and he surely must be, because all wealthy people were to some extent—then there was always the chance that he might think along the same lines as Andreas undoubtedly had: that she had descended into his household and befriended him because there had been something in it for her.

Would he believe it if she told him that she had only recently discovered his place in her life? Wouldn't he be inclined to be suspicious of her motives, considering she had not disclosed her identity immediately, had not thought to make initial contact via a letter? At least then she'd have given him the option of refusal.

Certainly, the firm foundation of their affection and friendship would be eroded by the revelation. How could it not be? And there was no way that she was prepared to jeopardise what they had, even if it meant keeping silent. When the time came for her to find alternative employment, she would find it close by so that she could continue visiting him and having him in her life. She would be his daughter in everything but name.

And what she now had with Andreas was even more of a reason to keep silent, although when she tried to disentangle her thoughts on that one, so that she could make sense of them, she could feel herself getting muddled and lost. It was like walking through a leafy archway only to discover that the bower led to a maze with frightening side-shoots and confusing, scary dead-ends.

It seemed safer to avoid the leafy archway, and she did that by keeping their sexual adventures completely separate from their working relationship. Holding him at bay afforded her an opportunity of control, which she badly needed. If she didn't take it he would walk all over her, taking what he wanted, and then dropping her from a great height the second he became bored. It seemed important to protect herself against when that time came. She just couldn't afford to let him see how deeply involved she was, how her emotions were all over the place. She was in free fall—and exposing her real identity… Well, what was worse than free fall? She couldn't think, but she knew how she could buy a first-class ticket there, and it would involve baring her soul, telling him who she really was and why she had made the move to Somerset to be with James.

She surfaced from her thoughts to find that he had covered the distance across the office to perch on the side of her desk, swamping her with his suffocating, addictive presence.

'Since you're the one who is so hell-bent on keeping our lives compartmentalised, then you won't be offended when I tell you that traipsing in whenever you feel like it isn't the professional approach I'm paying you for.'

'That's hardly fair!'

'"Hardly fair" is your hands-off policy during working hours. Why are you late?'

'I was with James's nutritionist. We were trying to devise salt-free, tempting options for him because he's been complaining about the blandness of his food.' She didn't raise her eyes above thigh level, but even the sight of that straining fabric only inches away from her arm made the hairs on the back of her neck stand on end. Memory was certainly a fickle friend. Right now she could have done without the memory of Andreas last night, with the silver moonlight washing through the windows of his bedroom silhouetting his perfect body as it moved against hers, straining as he took them to a climax that had left her half-sobbing.

'Thrilling. Did you come up with anything?' His sharp eyes hadn't missed the nervous way her pink tongue flicked out to lick her lips or the way her breathing had quickened.

'One or two interesting ideas. To be honest, the time just sort of ran away, hence I'm a few minutes late.'

'Forty-five.'

'But I made sure that the Matheson stuff you asked me to do was all emailed to you.'

'When did you get round to doing that?' He swung himself away from the desk and sauntered back to his own chair. 'When I left you, you didn't seem in any fit state to start compiling figures.' He shot her a wolfish smile, and her stomach flipped over as she weakly yielded to staring at his darkly charismatic face.

'I couldn't sleep,' she managed a little breathlessly. Her mind had been too busy, not least with the depressing thought of how deeply involved she had become with Andreas and the dire consequences it held for her. Working had been her feeble attempt to divert her brain from its one-track ruminations.

'So you decided to work? I hope I'm not rubbing off on you,' he drawled. 'I do recall you have strong feelings about workaholics.'

Elizabeth looked at him reproachfully over the top of her computer and he grinned back at her. His black mood had disappeared; it pleased him to think that she hadn't been able to sleep because he had been on her mind. It was a place he was more than happy to occupy.

'There's something I've been meaning to talk to you about.'

'Oh yes? Is it concerning work?'

'Of course it's concerning work,' Andreas said irritably. 'You've made it more than clear that that's the only topic of conversation permitted within the hallowed walls of this makeshift office. Pull up your chair.'

'Pull it up? Pull it up to where?'

'Pull it up to where I don't have to use a megaphone to be heard.' Andreas watched as she obligingly relocated her chair to the front of his desk. Much better. His eyes dropped to the shadow of her cleavage visible where the top two buttons of her white shirt were undone. It would take seconds to lock that office door so that he could explore the achingly familiar terrain under the businesslike outfit. The irony of him being the one who wanted to flout his own self-imposed rules of behaviour was not lost on him. Past experience had always had him as the one with stringent rules about boundary lines over which women could not step. He made love to them, entertained them, lavished them with presents—but he went to bed alone, and if work beckoned then they were always relegated to second place.

He certainly had never gritted his teeth at midnight when he was told that it was time for him to leave. He did now. Nor had he ever found himself doodling a woman's name on a piece of paper and then chucking the piece of crumpled paper in the bin with a mixture of guilt and annoyance. He did now. Hence what he saw as a fine solution to the problem.

'Have you given any thought to what happens next in your life plans?'

'My life plans?' Elizabeth gave a nervous laugh and looked at him hesitantly. 'I thought we were going to talk about work.'

'I'll get to that. But first answer my question. Thoughts about what happens next for you—any?'

'Not really.'

'Well, here's the good news, *I* have.' Andreas stood up, shoved his hands in his pockets and strolled to look out at the well-maintained gardens stretching out towards the open fields.

'Thank you, but there's really no need for you to work out life plans on my behalf,' Elizabeth told him lightly.

'Why not? From where I'm sitting, I wouldn't be surprised if you chose to put your life on hold just to stay here indefinitely.'

As there was no reply to that well-directed shot in the dark, Elizabeth maintained a cautious silence and waited to hear where this was going. *Nowhere good* was what her mind told her.

'But, of course, that would be utterly impractical. You're

young. All this...' he extended his hand to encompass the gloriously sweeping rural views '...might appeal for a while, but sooner or later the restrictions will begin to bear in on you. When that happens, when you start thinking about the months and the years of being buried out in the middle of nowhere...'

'Hardly *nowhere.* You make it sound as though a trip to the nearest town involves long-haul travel and inoculation shots!'

'You'll begin to crave the urgency of somewhere more lively. Not to mention the obvious fact that James will be able to manage on his own very shortly. His consultant says within the next month or so, bearing in mind he will have Maria here to attend to his catering and keep an eye on him.' Andreas paused and frowned, because there was no encouragement to be had in her down-bent head. 'Your role, to all intents and purposes, will be redundant.'

Tears gathered at the corners of her eyes and she blinked them away. 'Redundant' was such an awful word, implying a complete lack of use, no longer wanted or needed, superfluous to requirements. Having run for cover the minute those uncomfortable thoughts had presented themselves, Elizabeth cringed now at the brutality of the unavoidable reality.

'Ah, yes. I can see you've already given the matter some thought. Fortunately for you, I have a solution to hand.'

'A solution?'

'Of course.' A small smile of satisfaction curved Andreas's wide, sensuous mouth. 'Come with me to London.'

'*Come with you to London?*' This was about the last thing Elizabeth had expected to hear, and she stared at him open-mouthed while her sluggish brain tried to decipher the missing connections.

'It's as easy as that. I won't be staying here for ever and I want to take you with me.'

'But...but don't you already have a secretary? In London?

What will you do with her? Aren't there laws protecting people from unfair dismissal?'

'I'm not going to dismiss anyone,' Andreas said impatiently. 'What are you talking about? You won't be coming with me in the capacity of secretary. I already have my own personal assistant, and in turn she has her own people working for her. Believe me, when it comes to getting my orders followed through, there is no lack of highly efficient staff. Why do you think it has been possible for me to take time out and transfer my operations here for a while?'

'You mean you want me to come as your…?'

'Lover.' He strolled towards her and leaned down, hands on either side of her chair, caging her in so that the heady scent of him filled her nostrils, destabilising her; for a few seconds she really didn't quite take in what he was saying. When it filtered through, she blinked in alarm and placed her hands on his chest to push him away from her.

'You want me to give up everything here so that I can become your *mistress?*'

'Give *everything* up? In six weeks' time, there will be nothing *to* give up. You don't expect to be paid for hanging around, enjoying the countryside, do you?'

'No, of course not.'

'And I can understand why you maybe don't like the term "mistress"—so why don't we just say that what I want is for us to continue with what we have? And it'll be good…' His voice was husky and he raked his fingers through his hair while trying to gauge her reaction through narrowed eyes. He should have known that it was all in the phrasing, and that someone as inherently romantic as Elizabeth would want his request to sound a little less bald. But Andreas had never done romance.

'This is the wrong place to be having this sort of conversation,' he muttered, shooting her a darkly accusing look, as though she had been the one to instigate it.

'I can't come and *live* with you, Andreas!' The thought of it, however, was wickedly attractive. Wrong and dangerous, but still wickedly attractive. Just as having this relationship with him was wickedly attractive. Her common sense had gone on holiday and in its place was a reckless, devil-may-care foolishness that threatened her on every front.

'Why not? You would have everything you wanted and we would no longer have to wait until the house was quiet so that I could sneak into your bedroom like a randy teenager with his parents in the room next door.'

'What would I do, when you're off running your companies? Skulk in your apartment getting myself ready for when you returned?'

'Why are you picking holes in this? The sex between us is great. No, better than great. I want it to carry on. Simple solution for a simple problem.'

'And what happens when the *simple problem* no longer exists? What happens when you get bored with the arrangement?'

'Why attempt to cross bridges before they appear on the horizon?'

'Because that's the kind of boring person that I am,' Elizabeth said painfully. 'I like to be prepared.' She did. Coming to Somerset had been the only unpredictable thing she had ever done in her life. Of course, it had been worth it, because meeting her father had been a blessing, but on other fronts she had paid dearly for her unpredictability. This past week had made sense of all her stolen glances and unbidden excitement. She had fallen in love with Andreas, the man now standing there and coolly telling her that he had worked out a solution to the *simple problem* of wanting her: move in, have fun then move out. Hell, something should have prepared her for that.

'So do I,' Andreas agreed smoothly. 'Except when it comes to sex. Then I find unpredictability much more appetising. And why are you giving me a hard time over this?'

'I'm not giving you a hard time. I just… It's just not a very good idea.'

'Because you're not attracted to me?'

'You know that's not the case,' Elizabeth muttered, reddening.

'I know.' That small crack in the arguments she had generated, which had set his teeth on edge, was something he could work with. Like it or not, he wanted her, and he always got what he wanted; that was a simple fact.

He moved to where she was frozen to her chair and stood in front of her so that she was obliged to finally raise her eyes to meet his. He felt a surge of hot, primal satisfaction at what he saw lurking grudgingly in the green depths. She might talk the talk, but that was where it ended. She wanted him as much as he wanted her and, if she wanted him to dress up the starkness of his offer a little bit, then he was willing to go along with that.

He trailed one long finger across her cheek and then squatted down so that they were on eye level.

'I'm no good with flowery words,' he delivered with an honesty that wrenched at her heart strings—because his honesty made him vulnerable, whether he knew that or not, and Andreas didn't *do* vulnerable. 'But for me, asking you to share my space, to wake up with me and go to bed with me? Well, it's a pretty big deal.' His finger dipped to her lips, tracing their full outline, then moving on to linger in the hollow of her neck. She was barely aware when he reached behind to unravel her hair from its thick plait which hung down her back like copper rope, then he riffled his fingers through it and breathed huskily that that was much better.

'What—what are you doing?' Elizabeth stammered as she watched her carefully drawn boundaries, the boundaries that protected her, being plundered. 'We agreed that we wouldn't…'

'I agreed nothing of the sort.' He didn't rush as he went to the door and locked it. Elizabeth spun round as that definitive click sent a shiver of forbidden excitement and dread coursing through her veins. She wondered how she could have been naive enough to think that a man like Andreas—hot, passionate, accustomed to getting his own way—would politely give in to her rules. She stood up, reminding herself that when she was in this office she was no longer his lover but his employee—but, when she opened her mouth to tell him that, nothing came out but an inaudible croak. She watched him draw the curtains, instantly plunging the room into semi-darkness.

'We should be working…' she said breathlessly as he strolled towards her, as relaxed and as determined as a tiger moving in on its cornered prey.

'Yes, I know, but I'm willing to break all my own rules. For you.' His fabulous dark eyes glittered with intent and heat pooled in the pit of her stomach. She was mesmerised by the flare of passion in his eyes and, like a moth to a flame, she took a couple of steps towards him, reaching out and then stifling a moan of response as he pulled her to him.

Andreas felt a powerful surge of possession as his mouth descended on hers. She had offered half-hearted protests, and it was to her credit that she hadn't leapt at his generous suggestion that she accompany him back to London when the time came for him to take his leave, but her acquiescence now felt good.

He continued to kiss her as he propelled her the short distance to his desk, at which point he effortlessly lifted her so that she was sitting on the desk in front of him.

'One of my fantasies,' he said hoarsely as he unbuttoned her white shirt with unsteady fingers. 'My desk in London is as big as a bed, but I've never wondered what it would be like to see my woman splayed out naked on it.'

Elizabeth's brain snagged on the 'my woman' bit of the sentence and stayed there for a few seconds, savouring the possessiveness of it before letting it go, because even dwelling on that was a really bad idea.

'And yet…' shirt unbuttoned, Andreas set to work on her bra, which was a lot less fiddly '…with you, it's pretty much been on my mind every second that we've sat in here working together.' Released from their flimsy restraint, her lush breasts made him breathe in sharply.

He was familiar with her body in the most intimate way possible, yet was not immune to its magnificence every time he saw her naked. He couldn't get enough of her, but he couldn't explain why that was, except that maybe his diet had been a bit over-rich in tall, leggy, skinny blondes and that someone with womanly curves was an irresistible dish of the day.

Nor could he adequately explain to himself how it was that he could on the one hand tell himself that she was too great an unknown quantity—which was always a bad thing as far as he was concerned—and on the other hand still want her so much that it physically hurt.

Like now. Stripped bare from the waist up, he pushed her gently back so that she was lying on the desk, her legs dangling over the side, then he paused so that he could devour her hungrily with his eyes.

Having never known what it was like to have the power to command at her fingertips, she had fast discovered that it was a power she liked. She really enjoyed the way his dark, gleaming gaze dwelled on her with such rampant, masculine appreciation. He made her feel a hundred feet tall and yet as dainty as a kitten. With him, she could become mistress and slave at the same time.

Right now he was holding her captive as he explored her breasts with his hands and mouth. It was heady, lying prone on his desk half-naked while he was still fully clothed, albeit with his sleeves roughly rolled up to his elbows.

'Please, Andreas…' she whimpered, as his tongue grazed her nipple, a prelude to the erotic, warm invasion by his mouth as he began sucking hard, sending a spasm of pure pleasure shooting right through her.

'Please…what?'

'Take your clothes off.'

'When I'm good and ready, my darling.' He pinned her restless hands to her side, so that she was helpless against him, and in response she arched back to meet his questing mouth, pushing her breast against him, urging him on and spiralling into giddy heights of satisfaction as he aggressively made exquisite love to her breasts.

When she could take it no more, he ripped down her underwear in one smooth movement, and she cried out as he covered her stomach with his hand, easing down until he slipped his fingers into her and teased her moistness over and over, rubbing as he continued to lavish his wet caresses to the tightened bud of her nipple.

Only then did he break away so that he could yank off his clothes, although he didn't take his eyes off her heated body for a single instant. He had taught her to be proud of her body, and he liked the way she didn't try to hide herself; of course, she knew how much he enjoyed revelling in her womanly curves. Everything about her acted on him like a powerful aphrodisiac, even the way she feasted her eyes on his body, and that soft moan she gave as he touched his erect manhood, drawing her attention to his rampant erection. Later, but not here, she would taste it. The thought of that was almost enough to incite ejaculation.

Stilling that runaway anticipation, Andreas parted her legs and knelt like a supplicant before her so that he could do what he had wanted to do every time she had sat in front of him dutifully taking notes with no idea about what he had been thinking.

Elizabeth's breathing quickened and then she held her breath expectantly, releasing it on a sigh of mindless pleasure as he began licking her, expertly finding the place where just the slightest pressure was sufficient to send her into sexual orbit.

When he finally thrust into her, she was already at such a peak of excitement that it took only seconds for her to explode with an orgasm that left her as weak and boneless as a rag doll. Reality penetrated very slowly as Andreas stood up and looked down at her with a smile.

'Fantasy fulfilled,' he murmured, turning to rescue his hastily discarded clothes from the ground. 'And, for once, imagination was not a patch on the reality. I never realised that a desk could be so multi-functional.'

Elizabeth slid off the wretched multi-functional desk with a cold sense of muted panic, forced to acknowledge that the very last of her painstakingly erected defences lay in ruins around her. Her hands were trembling as she flung her clothes back on. For Andreas, this would have been a little amusing romp, a little sex-fantasy fulfilled. For her, the enormity of what she had done was crashing down on her like a ton of bricks. Against her will, and totally against her better judgement, love had crept up on her but at least she had been able to project some semblance of control. Now what? Was she to become his sex object with a few employee-duties thrown in? It was within his power to destroy what she had built with James, should he choose to do so, and foolishly she had granted him that power and more. She frankly only had herself to blame.

She couldn't bring herself to look at him when she was finally fully dressed and back at her desk.

'So…' Andreas sat on the edge of the desk with an expression closely resembling that of a cat in full possession of the cream. 'Proof positive of why London with me would be such a good idea. I never thought I'd hear myself say this, but I'm a big enough man to admit that whatever spell you've managed to weave over me…' He pushed himself off the desk and sauntered across to the window, idly surveying the grounds before turning round to face her. 'Well, I'm very happy to let you carry on weaving it.'

Elizabeth mentally added a couple of vital clauses to that statement: 'Until I get bored' was the first, and 'at which point I won't expect you to hang around my godfather, as you'll be history' was the second.

'You don't seem to have understood, Andreas—I won't be coming to London with you. I know your godfather won't need me here for ever, and I've already decided that when that time comes in a few weeks' time I'm going to look for a job locally. I like it here. I like the big, open spaces. I like to think that the coast isn't a million miles away. London holds nothing for me any more.'

That they had just finished sharing earth-shattering sex, that he had repeated his offer—which, from where he was sitting, was the best offer she was likely to come across in her lifetime—and that she had politely but firmly turned him down left Andreas speechless. He had even been willing to go against his instincts, to overlook the niggling doubts about her motivation for being in James's life. Rejection was an unfamiliar taste, and one which brought all his inherent sense of pride slamming into place.

The smile died from his lips and he looked at her through cool, narrowed eyes. It was not in his nature to beg, and to try and coax her out of her stubborn, idiotic decision constituted begging. He shrugged and walked across to his desk where he proceeded to reboot his computer.

'Your choice,' he dismissed lazily.

Faced with his immediate acceptance of her refusal, and perversely gutted by the fact that he hadn't even attempted to talk her out of it, it struck her that she now no longer knew what her role in his life was to be. The thought of 'nothing' opened up a gaping, black void that filled her with terror.

'I…I hope this doesn't make working together difficult.'

His mobile rang, and as he reached for it he looked at her without a change of expression. He could have been a stranger. 'Why should it? You do a good job. The sex was a bonus.'

A *bonus?* Elizabeth opened her mouth to protest at the arrogance of that statement, but he was frowning into his phone with a tight-lipped, shuttered face and she realised that she was dismissed from the conversation. And if she hadn't got the message then, she certainly did when he placed his hand briefly over his mobile and nodded at the door.

'Private call. Why don't you take the afternoon off? If I need you, I'll let you know.' With which he swivelled his chair away so that she exited the room with as little ceremony as she had entered it many weeks ago.

CHAPTER SEVEN

ELIZABETH saw nothing further of Andreas for the remainder of the day. He hadn't summoned her to work and she had no intention of loitering by the office door, waiting for his call. In her heart, she understood that her duties as secretary were over and she was shocked at how deeply she felt the loss—quite apart from the loss of him. It was left to her to offer a mumbling explanation to James over dinner that she probably wouldn't be working for his godson in the afternoons, and she vaguely fabricated something about Andreas probably returning to London.

'Shame,' James said, his blue eyes a little too shrewdly fixed on her face for comfort. 'Guess you'll miss that. There's been a lightness in your step these past few weeks.' She stammered, uncomfortably, that she had no idea what he was talking about, but her face was beetroot-red and she didn't like the way his eyes twinkled and his lips twitched. She didn't care for the way he had made a big show of changing the conversation; James, notoriously, could hang on to a subject like a dog with a bone and chew it to death. 'I know what's going on, my girl' that bull-in-china-shop change of conversation seemed to shout, 'and I won't embarrass you by pursuing it'.

For the first time, dinner was awkward, with Andreas's seat

glaringly empty; where he was, she had no idea. She tried very hard to smile and act normal, but the questions in her head which she had damped down for so long rose up demanding answers. Her clear-cut plan of getting to know James, and gently breaking her true relationship with him when his health improved, had been thrown into disarray by Andreas's unexpected presence—then further obliterated by their growing emotional entanglement. The fact that they had become lovers had been the icing on the cake, for falling in love with him had been step one in her dramatic change of direction.

The following morning, she half-expected to discover that he had already returned to London, but just in case he was still around—and not knowing what to do about appearing at the office at the usual time—Elizabeth took the coward's way out and inveigled a day off. She took James for his usual visit to the tea shop so that he could enjoy his weekly round of grumpy flirting with Dot Evans. This had progressed into the occasional evening meeting when Dot had visited the house, bearing cake and flowers and ignoring James's disgruntled accusation that flowers and cakes made him feel like an invalid.

She decided she would then spend the remainder of the day exploring a couple of nearby towns because Dot had kindly offered to return 'this crotchety old man'—'Heaven knows how you put up with him!'—back to the house.

And, just in case Andreas did expect her to resume duties in the afternoon, she had cleared her workload and would kindly leave James to pass on the message.

'Can't tell him yourself?' James barked over his scone and cup of tea, drawing attention to himself, as he usually managed to do in the tea shop. 'Since when do you need a go-between? Don't tell me you're suddenly scared of that godson of mine, my girl? Wouldn't believe it if you did. Heard the way you answer him back—wonderful!'

There was some mumbling about poor service-network for her mobile phone in outlying rural areas, and other random excuses that sounded feeble even to her own ears.

But now, free to explore the countryside, which she had done precious little of over the last month or two, Elizabeth found things to be lacklustre. She went through the motions of trying to enjoy her day off, but her mind continued to gnaw away at all her misery and uncertainties and zoom in on a tortuous circle of self-blame and regret.

Furthermore, she had no idea what she was going to say to Andreas when she next met him, and the prospect of that meeting was enough to send her pulses racing and her stomach twisting into sickening knots. By three, she was more than ready to head back to the house, but she forced herself to linger a little bit longer so that it was a little after five by the time she eventually turned the corner of the single-track road that led to it. She had been given the use of the little runaround used by Maria for errands in the village, and the car seemed as relieved to be back in its familiar surroundings as she was, strangely enough.

She drove into the enormous courtyard, and the first hint that something wasn't quite right was the jaunty red sports-car skewed at an angle in front of the house.

Cautiously, Elizabeth let herself in through the kitchen door and, having scuttled past some empty rooms, was easily on the home stretch to her own bedroom when a woman's voice stopped her dead in her tracks.

'You!'

The accent was pure-bred cut glass, and seething with venom. Very slowly Elizabeth turned round, and her startled green eyes met with icy-blue chips narrowed with hostility. The woman standing in front of her with her hands on her hips was the most drop-dead-beautiful woman Elizabeth had ever seen in her entire life. She wore a dove-grey trouser suit, and in her high heels must have stood at six foot at the very least. Wind swept, fed up and devoid of make-up, Elizabeth's already fast-fading self-confidence took an immediate nose dive as she hovered uncertainly with her hand on the banister.

'Me?' A quick glance around told her that she surely was the one being addressed as there was no one else in the hall. She cleared her throat while her brain continued to process the woman's amazing beauty. She had the body of a gazelle, and poker-straight blond hair, of the type Elizabeth had always secretly yearned for, swung around her perfect face in a sharply cut, graduated bob. Had it not been for the scowl, the woman could have been described as having the face of an angel, from the blond hair and blue eyes to the rosebud mouth and fine, arched eyebrows.

'I *know* what's been going on here.'

'Sorry?' Elizabeth took a couple of small steps back, because physical injury seemed to be a possibility.

'Andreas's told me everything!'

'Who *are* you?' With a rapidly beating heart, she began to mount the staircase, while searching for divine rescue from one of the many doors leading out of the hall.

'I'm Andreas's girlfriend—or rather I *was* until he got it into his head that it might be a good idea to start sleeping with the staff.'

Elizabeth could feel her face drain of colour as guilt, shame and anger burst inside her like a boil being lanced.

'You're his *girlfriend?*' Andreas had been sleeping with *her* while he had had a girlfriend? And not just any girlfriend—one who looked as though she had stepped straight off the cover of *Vogue!* The laughter and passion they had shared, the camaraderie working together in his makeshift office, suddenly evolved into a stark, bitter scenario of a bored man stuck out in the sticks deciding that a little bit of sex might brighten up the tedium. In London he would sleep with the model, and in Nowhereland he would share his bed with the plain Jane for comic relief.

Elizabeth had never felt so mortified in her entire life. If the ground had chosen to open up in front of her, she would gladly have jumped right in.

'He broke up with you because of *me?*' The words were wrenched out of her as she desperately tried to salvage some dignity from the situation.

'He broke up with me because he happened to be here and *you* were more convenient—on tap, so to speak!'

Elizabeth spun round and began fumbling her way up the stairs. She wondered if that was Andreas's version of events—that he had taken the easy option, the one *on tap,* so to speak. After all, it wasn't as though either she or his girlfriend had any emotional ties with him. And maybe he had been amused at the novelty of bedding a woman he wouldn't have looked at in a million years under normal circumstances. How many times had he laughed and told her how unique she was? 'Unique' now seemed a description that covered a wide range of qualities, none of them flattering. A three-headed dog would be unique, but you wouldn't want to share your life with one.

And hadn't life-sharing been there at the back of her mind? A crazy little notion that had given her an illicit thrill late at night after he had returned to his bedroom, leaving behind him his scent, the indentation of his body on her bed, the intangible reminder of his presence.

With her hand on the door to her room, she turned to see that the woman had followed her up the stairs.

'I guess you think you've won?'

'I think maybe we've both been losers.'

'Don't even *try* to lump me in the same boat as you. Look at you—you're…you're not even anything to look at!'

Elizabeth had to crane her neck upwards to meet the blonde's eyes. She felt very calm now in the face of that insult.

'I may not be much to look at, but I would never chase after a man who'd dumped me,' she said quietly. 'Does Andreas even know that you're here?'

'Of course he knows! I telephoned him yesterday.' The cut-glass accent was thick with scorn. 'In fact, I think it's safe to say that seeing me will probably remind him of what he's been missing. You may have had him because you made yourself available—and in this neck of the woods why not take what was on offer?—but believe me, sweetie, Andreas's heading back to civilization, and you won't be joining him.'

'I know that,' Elizabeth whispered without thinking. 'And so does he. I've already told him.'

'What's that?'

'Andreas. He asked me to move in with him and I turned him down.' She laughed bitterly. 'Best thing I ever did. So you're welcome to him! And good luck to you both. You deserve each other.' She opened the door but got no further than sticking one foot inside the bedroom, because she found that the blonde's long, manicured fingers had reached out to grip the side of the door.

'He asked you to *move in with him?*'

'I don't want to talk about this. Please. Just go.'

'He asked *you* to move in with him? Why would he do that? He told me about you, how you just appeared here from nowhere…' The blue eyes were narrowed menacingly on Elizabeth's ashen face. 'He would never have asked you to share his house. Never.'

She turned around and stalked off down the corridor, leaving Elizabeth staring at the erect back and feeling weirdly as though she had been catapulted into a horror movie, one in which everyone knew the lines except her.

Where had the blonde disappeared to? To Andreas's room? Was he there?

What would be the point of him hanging around now? James was virtually back to his old self, and if he had been inclined to prolong his stay because of her then that reason was no more. Besides, wasn't the blonde right? Next to her, Elizabeth was as physically appealing as a piece of mouldy cheese.

She forced herself to have a very long bath, to wash her hair and then blow-dry it, in the hope that by the time she finally showed her face downstairs Andreas and the witch might have already left. The house was so quiet at seven, when she eventually went to the sitting room to find James, that she almost started believing her own piece of fiction.

It was therefore with some shock that she pushed open the sitting-room door to find both Andreas and James sitting in frozen silence opposite one another.

'We have company!' James barked, glaring at his godson. 'Some stray vermin managed to find its way into my house.'

'Do you mean the blonde?' She had imagined that she would be wracked with nerves, coming face to face with Andreas, but in fact she felt icy calm. 'I know. I met her. Apparently—' she stared at Andreas without flinching '—she's your girlfriend.' Elizabeth was gratified to see him flush darkly, and she moved to stand behind James with her hands on his shoulders because she needed the additional moral support. 'You should have mentioned her to me, Andreas. I'm sure she would have enjoyed visiting.'

'She's visited,' Andreas said abruptly, standing up to help himself to another drink from the wine decanter on the table. 'And now she's on her way back to London.'

Elizabeth was further enraged to notice just how cool and

composed he was, whilst she was seething with anger and finding it hard to control her shaking.

'Surely that's a bit rough? I'm sure there'll be enough supper to go round…'

'You're overstepping your brief,' Andreas said in a clipped voice. 'When I want your thoughts on possible dinner-guests, I'll ask for them. And I've spent long enough discussing Amanda with my godfather, so why don't you tell me where you've been all day?'

'Relaxing.'

'Do I pay you to relax?'

'My workload was up to date. I felt like I needed a break.' She received a morale-boosting squeeze of the hands from James, which didn't go unnoticed by Andreas. Foul mood that he was in, he glared at her. What, she wondered, did he have to glare about?

'Now, children! I'm too old to endure bickering, and I'm certainly too old to endure your totties racing down here, Andreas.'

'She's not my *totty,*' Andreas said through gritted teeth. 'Amanda and I were a done deal.'

Would that have been just about the time you decided you needed a change of scenery? Elizabeth wondered as jealousy bit through her. If James hadn't been there, she would have done more than just ask him that, because in the mood she was in she wanted to do more than just ask a bunch of questions to which she already knew the answers. She wanted to fling something hard and heavy at him. Never had she felt so shaken in her life before, and she knew why. Andreas had changed her and she didn't appreciate the change. She had morphed from an easy going, amiable person—a person who avoided mood swings and tried very hard to hang on to her composure; a person who had learnt great reserves of patience, having taken care of her mother for so long—into a firebrand. She found that she was clinging like a limpet to James's shoulder and she took a few deep breaths and moved around to sit down.

Would the conversation struggle towards normality? she wondered. While Amanda packed her case upstairs and vanished back towards London.

Elizabeth would never know the answer to that one because no sooner had she sat down—blessed relief for her legs which felt like jelly—than the door was pushed open and there was Amanda, framed in the doorway like an avenging angel.

The trouser suit was gone, replaced by a red dress that hugged her body like cling film. Elizabeth realised that, while Andreas had doubtless been in the sitting room trying to placate James, Amanda had taken the opportunity to have a bath and freshen up.

For a few seconds both James and Andreas seemed to be frozen to the spot. James disapproving and working himself up to one of his famous rants, and Andreas's hard features stamped with icy disdain. Elizabeth almost felt sorry for the woman because there was nothing Andreas loathed more than a scene, as he had once told her in passing. And Amanda certainly looked like a woman on the verge of causing a very big scene.

She stepped into the room and waved a bundle of papers at them, at which point Elizabeth felt the room begin to spin around her. She made to get up and then immediately collapsed back onto the sofa.

'Just thought you'd like to have a look at these!' She smiled triumphantly at Elizabeth. Between her grasping fingers, the faded blue envelopes were instantly recognisable.

'You have no right…'

'Oh, I think everyone in here will agree that I had every right to tell them exactly what you are! And I can't imagine what took you so long. Did you think that you needed to spend some time buttering the old man up before you staked your claim?' Amanda's china-blue eyes were cool, amused and smugly satisfied that pay-back time had arrived. 'Well, good luck.' She spun round without glancing in Andreas's direction. It was a magnificent spin, a neatly executed twirl which ensured that every aspect of her fabulous body was revealed, a timely reminder to her ex of what he would be missing.

Elizabeth had no time to feel jealous because she was way too busy feeling terrified. Her eyes were glued to the bundle of envelopes which had been casually dropped on the old, mahogany table in the middle of the room. On the one hand, she wanted nothing more than to dash to the table, snatch up the envelopes and run away as fast as she could. On the other hand, she was overcome by a sense of fatalism. What would be, would be.

She gradually became aware of both Andreas and James staring at her. Amanda had left with a flourish, although Elizabeth couldn't have said exactly when.

Andreas was the first to break the silence.

'Are you going to explain what the hell that was all about?' He glanced at the envelopes burning a hole on the table, and knew that all the vague suspicions he had entertained about her were now going to be proved. Little Miss Innocent looked as guilty as sin with her colour up and her fingers twisting restively on her lap.

'May I have a word with James privately?' Elizabeth ventured and Andreas shot her a look of rampant incredulity.

'Well, in that case…' She took the bundle of letters and handed them to James, along with his reading glasses, which were in the top pocket of his shirt and which he constantly forgot. 'Do you remember a woman called Phyllis? You met her, well, over twenty-five years ago. She was thirty-two at the time and you were in your late forties. She was crazy about you, except she didn't know at the time that you were already married…'

James looked at her on a sharply indrawn breath as his quick mind connected the dots, and he reached for the bundle of envelopes. His hand was shaking. 'I remember her,' he said quietly. 'I used to call her my vanilla milkshake, because of the colour of her hair and because she brought such sweetness and pleasure to my life.' Tears formed in the corners of his eyes and he rubbed them away with his fingers. 'Her nose was not unlike yours, my dear. I'm afraid I can't quite bring myself to read these just yet. May I hold on to them for a while?'

'I would have told you sooner.' Elizabeth knelt next to him and lowered her head. 'I so wanted to get to know you. Then when I discovered that you were ill, that your heart was weak… I kept putting it off, and then it seemed so big I was scared.' When she felt his old hand on her head, she breathed a sigh of relief. The tension of the past months of uncertainty were finally released in tears which she allowed to flow freely down her cheeks. From behind her, she could feel Andreas's eyes on her; she had no idea what he was thinking and she told herself fiercely that she didn't care. The only thing that mattered was that she was accepted by her father. But she *did* care.

'I'm sorry,' she mumbled, sniffing.

'So am I, my dear. But regret is a wasted emotion, so enough of that. Andreas, my boy, it's time to leave us be for a moment. We have a lot to discuss.'

It was two hours before Elizabeth emerged from the sitting room. James could still not bring himself to read the letters. She thought that he might read them in his room later, and in the privacy of his bedroom reflect on opportunities missed and chances wasted—although he had stood firm in his belief that there was nothing to be gained from regrets.

For her part, she felt wrung out but at peace for the first time, possibly in her life.

James had retired to bed. Maria would bring him supper on a tray, he had told her, clutching the letters as she helped him to his feet. Now Elizabeth headed for the kitchen. When she glanced through the arched, leaded side-window in the hall, she was distantly aware that the red sportscar had vanished along with its owner. It seemed ironic that the fallout maliciously anticipated by Amanda had transpired into an act of kindness.

She swung into the kitchen and there he was, standing with a drink in one hand and giving the impression that he had been there waiting for her all along, knowing that she would want a fortifying cup of coffee after the recent upheaval. Except that the expression on his face wasn't that of a man about to deliver a generous dose of sympathy and compassion.

Elizabeth stopped dead in her tracks and waited for her heart to stop beating wildly, but of course if didn't. All the while she had been talking to James, she had been sickeningly aware of the further confrontation to come with his godson. Even though she told herself that whatever he said would be meaningless, because she wasn't involved with him, and indeed had seen him for the man he really was—a man who picked up and dropped women without his conscience being bothered in any way. Amanda, dumped from a great height because he had discovered a newer toy, must have been distraught to have jumped in her car and driven all the way to Somerset for a showdown. It was crazy to see her as the bad guy, when the really bad guy was standing in front of her with an expression that could freeze water.

Elizabeth was far from confrontational, but on this occasion she decided that she would launch her attack before he had the opportunity to shoot her down in flames, which was what his glacial eyes promised. Going against her inclination to open her sentence with *I'm sorry, I know you must be furious; please try to understand the position I found myself in,* she said instead, 'You never told me that you had a girlfriend. Never!'

The shock and hurt she had felt came back to her with remembered force, bolstering her confidence. Bitterness and anger were two very strong allies. 'How could you? How could you string me along when you had a girlfriend in London? If I *had* decided to return to London with you—which I *wouldn't* have—then what were you going to do with Amanda? Stuff her in a cupboard somewhere? Or were you going to juggle two women at the same time?'

'I don't believe I'm hearing this.'

'You treat people as though they have no feelings, Andreas, and you do that because you have no feelings of your own.'

'You *dare* stand there and talk about how human beings should treat one another? Before you claim the moral high-ground, let me just remind you that you're a liar, and quite probably a gold-digger into the bargain.' And that was about the calmest way he could have phrased it. Never had he felt so shell-shocked in his life, and furious with himself that he had been taken in. Hadn't he known from the start that there was something fishy about her? And yet he had put all that to one side because he had been overtaken by something as utterly controllable as lust. In the presence of his godfather, he had been obliged to hang on to his restraint, but he had been saving his fury for when he caught her on her own. Did she think that she could wrong-foot him with a load of irrelevant questions about Amanda?

'Were you sleeping with her while you were planning to seduce me?'

Andreas flushed darkly. Somewhere along the line his so-called planned seduction had become mired in the very real, very powerful attraction he had felt, and that in itself enraged him.

'I don't believe I'm obliged to answer questions of that nature.'

'Well, why should *I* answer questions from you?' She stood her ground in the face of his blazing anger at her unprecedented insurrection.

Andreas was finding it hard to equate the stubborn creature with her arms folded with the timid girl who had first introduced herself into James's life. Into her *father's* life. Unwilling to release his anger, he coldly thought that that timidity was what had been required of her at the time.

'You came into this house in the guise of the caring assistant so that you could check out how the land lay,' he drawled in a remote, icy voice that she hated. 'And you tell me that you don't see why you should explain yourself to me? That's rich, coming from the woman who has felt free to stand on her soap box and preach to me about my so-called arrogance.'

'I'm not a hypocrite, if that's what you're implying.' But her balloon had burst and she could feel herself deflate. This was the man she loved, for better or worse, and speculating about what he thought of her was killing her.

'You came here under false pretences. How do I know that you are who you say you are? How do I know that you haven't been light-fingered with someone else's property?'

'I haven't. There are details about my mum that only I could know. Details that…that James knows as well. And I'm sorry about the false pretences. I would have said something a lot sooner, but…'

'But?' There was no point pursuing the doubt angle because she was telling the truth. Andreas could see that as clearly as he could see the fool he had unwittingly made of himself.

'First of all, I didn't want to upset James. And then it just got too complicated.'

'I find it hard to believe that there could be all that many complications attached to announcing your identity in view of all the fabulous wealth you stand to inherit.'

Elizabeth blanched and stepped back as though she had been struck. How easy it was for passion to turn to cold-blooded accusations and hatred; she heard the hatred even though he hadn't raised his voice. In Andreas's black-and-white world, she had deceived him, and in deceiving him had committed an unforgivable sin.

'I didn't come here because I thought that there might be something in it for me, and it's really horrible of you to suggest that. But then, I don't know why I should be surprised.'

Andreas's eyes tangled with her wide, green, disappointed gaze and something inside him shifted with exasperating ease. To think that he was feared and admired for his astounding self-control and ability to see things with dispassionate logic. It was pathetic!

'What's that supposed to mean?' It was a question he had not meant to ask, because just asking for any kind of clarification on the matter suggested weakness. 'Scratch that. I'm really not interested.'

Elizabeth gritted her teeth and inhaled deeply, because standing up to Andreas was like trying to keep upright in a force-ten gale. 'I'll tell you anyway,' she said in a rush, 'because you always think that you can say whatever you want to say and hang the consequences. You thought the worst of me the minute I got here; I don't know why I thought that getting to know me would have made you see that I'm not the kind of money-grabbing gold-digger you originally thought I was. I was stupid to think that you might have given me the benefit of the doubt.'

'Oh, please, spare me the violins! And don't try and pretend that you're purer than the driven snow. "False pretences" is what springs to mind. In other words, you *lied.* Liars don't have the privilege of giving speeches on other people's priniciples.'

'You should talk,' Elizabeth muttered.

'What do you intend to do now?' Andreas asked coldly, choosing to ignore her *sotto voce* remark.

Elizabeth's eyes skittered away from his shimmering, forbidding gaze. With every passing word, she could feel the doors slamming on the fragile relationship they had had. She had got in too deep and this was the price she was going to have to pay. 'I wasn't going to tell him!' she blurted out, and Andreas frowned, impatient and uncomprehending. 'I was going to keep my identity secret. I just wanted to get to know my father, and I would have been happy to leave it there.'

'You expect me to believe that?'

'No.'

Andreas found himself taken aback by the quietly spoken monosyllable, but he recovered quickly. 'How well you know me.' His mouth curled derisively. 'And you still haven't answered my question.'

Elizabeth shrugged. 'I know that James…my father…no longer really needs daily attention. He asked me to stay on here, but I've decided that I'm going to look for work locally, maybe rent somewhere in the village.'

'How noble of you. I wonder how long that ambition will last with the siren of a manor house calling? Rent free.'

Elizabeth lifted her chin and glared. 'I think I've answered enough of your questions!'

'You're right.' He astonished her by smoothly agreeing. 'But there are just a few little pearls of wisdom that I'm going to put your way, and if you have a single iota of sense you'll make damn sure you pay heed to them. The first is that, whatever your real motives are for approaching James in this manner, for getting under his skin and then revealing yourself in your true colours, *I* am not my godfather. I will leave for London in two days' time, but I have access online to all his financial dealings. I handle his considerable banking affairs, and if I spot *one* unaccounted for penny going astray I'll be on your case like a ton of bricks.'

So now she was a common thief? Andreas scowled, stamping down a hitherto unseen side to him that appeared gullible enough to find that notion laughable. He reminded himself that not only was the woman a liar and a fraud but she was also the woman who had turned him down. Narrow escape for him, naturally, but he was still outraged at the rejection.

Elizabeth nodded because she was weary of repeating her intentions. Her brain had latched on to that simple statement that he would be leaving for London in two days, and having latched on was refusing to let it go. She could already feel the emptiness of his imminent departure swirling around her like a wintry breeze, even though she told herself that their relationship had only ever been an interlude that would come to an end, and that as endings went sooner was surely better than later.

'Needless to say,' Andreas informed her coolly, 'your services with me are no longer required.'

Like the hired help, which was what Amanda had called her, she was now being dismissed.

She turned away, tears blurring her vision, though fortunately her long hair, cascading around her face, hid that final humiliation from his piercing eyes.

She couldn't bring herself to look at him as she left the kitchen. All her energy seemed to have seeped out of her body, and it was only as she was tiredly heading up the stairs that she realised that she would have some contact with him in time to come, as James's godson. Limited contact, granted, but any contact would require some measure of self-composure. She just couldn't fall to pieces every time she looked at his face, heard his voice or allowed her eyes to linger on the sinewy lines of his body. She would go mad.

She would have to work hard at getting him out of her system. Now that everything was out in the open, she would be able to really get to know her father, to find out all she could about him, and to indulge him in a way she had not been able to when she had just been his carer. That would go a long way to restoring her sanity and putting the sorry situation with Andreas into perspective. In due course, she told herself, it would likewise help to patch up the wear and tear on her heart—and if the patch-up job was a bit dodgy to start with then over time it would become more solid, and eventually to the casual observer it would look as if it had never been damaged.

Maybe she would step out of her vacuum and actually begin living a little. Maybe she would start taking an interest in guys. Maybe she was just kidding herself when she assumed that Andreas was irreplaceable. How could someone so arrogant, so merciless, so emotionally deep-frozen, be irreplaceable? It didn't make sense.

She needed to recapture the practical girl she had been all her life and then everything would fall into place.

She wasn't to know that that was not going to be an option.

CHAPTER EIGHT

WITH the whirring of the helicopter blades making conversation on his mobile impossible, Andreas finally had time to think about what was happening back at the manor house—after a week of plunging himself back into a work routine which even for him had been extreme, and had left his secretary dazed and exhausted. None of it was to his liking.

High on the list of reasons for his ongoing foul temper was the fact that he hadn't been able to rid his mind of Elizabeth. She kept popping up like the proverbial bad penny at the least opportune moments: in the middle of high-level meetings. On the date he had had with a supermodel of the leggy-blonde format. In the middle of writing a report. Even at the gym, where he had lost concentration and remarkably ceded a pretty easy squash match to his partner.

Since when had he ever been the kind of guy who lost sleep over a woman? He had lost sleep over *her,* and he just didn't get it. Had she put some kind of crazy spell on him? It felt like it. Except Andreas didn't believe in crazy spells. God knew, it was a simple enough situation. Guy meets girl; guy distrusts girl; guy sleeps with girl; girl turns out to be liar, cheat and who knew what else? Guy makes his thoughts known and washes his hands of situation because no woman was worth the headache. Easy. Sorted. So why had she succeeded in taking up residence in his head like a squatter with no intention of clearing off? He couldn't understand it.

And now this.

He scowled and stared out at a countryside that was moving past at dizzying speed and was barely visible under the cloak of darkness. He had instant and unpleasant recall of every word of the conversation he had had with his godfather the day before.

James had been on top of the world ever since Amanda's startling revelation, and Andreas had endured so many conversations on the subject of his new-found lease of life that anyone would have been forgiven for thinking that his godfather had personally been the witness to a miracle of biblical proportions.

So it should have come as no surprise that trumpeting his happiness to the rest of the world would be on the agenda. Yet Andreas had been dumbfounded at James's chipper announcement that he was having a bash, a rather substantial bash, to introduce his daughter to the great and the good.

'I thought you had no time for the great and the good,' Andreas had remarked, softening the clipped disapproval in his voice by adding, 'You always maintained that they were a bunch of phonies only to be tolerated because of Portia and her never-ending social climbing.'

But apparently Elizabeth had changed all that.

'I can't wait to show off my beautiful girl,' James had crowed with obvious glee. 'I'm hoping you will make it to the party, Andreas. You and Elizabeth,' he had continued slyly, 'seemed so in tune with one another that I cannot believe that you haven't been down already.'

'It's been a week, James, and I've had to hit the ground running here.'

Which was why he had excused himself from attending any party. Certainly events of that nature bored the living daylights out of him. So what the hell was he doing now, dressed to the nines like an advertisement for Italian tailoring, in his helicopter? He thought of Elizabeth luxuriating in the spotlight, despite all her protests about just wanting to get to know her father, and his scowl intensified. Of course he had planned on returning to Somerset, and had vaguely assumed that once his visit was announced Elizabeth would conveniently make herself scarce. Yet when he thought of her making herself scarce he was infuriatingly aware of a tightness in his chest that was close to a physical pain. He didn't get it. He just knew that he had gone from being a man in total control of everything around him to a man driven by needs and cravings, that were making a nonsense of the cool-headed logic that was pivotal to his well-ordered universe.

'Five minutes, sir.'

Andreas grunted. By the time he made it to the manor, the party would already be in full swing, and he had no doubt that Elizabeth would be living it up as the belle of the ball. For a girl from the wrong side of the tracks, she had suddenly hit the jackpot, and wouldn't she be enjoying the experience?

Not to mention the thrill of mixing with the sons, nephews and friends of friends of the great and the good, among whom there was certainly a suitor in waiting.

Another little aside which James had confided almost as an afterthought at the end of their conversation.

'I wouldn't want her to become bored out here,' James had said in a wistful voice, which was so unlike him that Andreas had had to bite back the urge to be sarcastic. 'And what better way of staving off boredom for a girl than to have some suitable lad in the background?'

'You don't know any *suitable lads,*' Andreas had felt compelled to point out as his mind grappled with the disconcerting vision of Elizabeth in bed with another man. He hadn't bothered to conceal the sudden chill in his voice as jealousy had taken root, primitive, bone-breaking jealousy that made him clench his jaw in angry rejection.

'But I know people who do! In fact, you'd be surprised,' James had added smugly, 'how many people want to come and see the wealthy hermit and his daughter. Nothing like a good scandal to get people crawling out of the woodwork! Dot's been handling the whole thing, and never mind that it's all last minute. Calendars are being cleared faster than you can say Bollinger! Never thought I'd be having so much fun at my ripe old age.'

A driver had been arranged to bring his car down from London and chauffeur him from air field to manor, but even in the back of the silent car—when Andreas could feasibly have used the down time to make a few business calls—he had found his mind too busily engaged in the situation that lay ahead.

It was ludicrous to think that Elizabeth would allow herself to be pushed into going on a series of dates with James's idea of eligible bachelors. Andreas had met several of those over the years at parties, when Portia had been around, and they were usually neatly split into two categories: the chinless wonders with titles, and the pushy yuppies with money. He couldn't credit that Elizabeth would find either appealing, but doubtless she would feel obliged to give them house room because she wouldn't want to disappoint James.

That set his teeth on edge. To distract himself from his unpleasant train of thought, he fiddled with his phone, sliding his finger over the surface and idly scanning his address book—pausing fractionally when he got to Isobel's name, but he had no inclination to call the newly acquired blonde. He wasn't entirely sure what had possessed him to go on a date with her in the first place. She made great arm-candy but her conversation had been simpering, the date had been lukewarm and he was already aware that she would regrettably have to be jettisoned. He was finding it hard to remember those peaceful times when work had been everything and great arm-candy had been a revitalising tonic.

He stuck the phone back in his pocket and felt his incipient bad mood go up a notch as his limo began weaving slowly down the familiar country lanes that led to James's house. Nor did it improve when the car turned the corner and he was rewarded with the sight of blazing lights, a courtyard festooned with outdoor heaters and massive urns of flowers and an array of cars that stretched around the rim of the courtyard and down the long lane that led up to the house. People were milling around outside, smoking. He was visibly reminded of the parties Portia used to give in her heyday, parties to which he had been invited only at James's insistence: music, dancing, food, champagne, name-dropping and networking on a scale that would make your head spin.

'Drop me here.' He leaned forward to tap his driver on the shoulder. 'And take the car back up to London. I'll make my own way back.'

'Are you sure, sir?'

'The pub in the town does an excellent meal, and there are rooms there if you don't want to make the trip tonight. Use my name and sign the bill.' With that he let himself out of the car and seriously began to question the rashness of his decision to disobey his very logical, highly controlled streak which had told him to stay in London and let them both get on with the business of blazing her name in neon lights all over the county.

Elizabeth, just at that moment passing one of the windows that overlooked the courtyard and the long, straight avenue that led towards the lane at the end, missed the tall figure striding up to the house with his hands shoved into his pockets and a grim expression on his face.

She was busily trying to make herself as background as was humanly possible for someone wearing red. With heels. And hair artfully straightened by the local hairdresser and falling to her waist. She had been dreading this party; she had done her very best to talk her father out of it, had protested on every possible front, but in the end had caved in because he had been so ridiculously excited at the prospect of it. Reading between the lines, she had glimpsed a man who under his gruff, sometimes brutal 'let's call a spade a spade' demeanour had been vulnerable over the years to whispers about his childless state—murmurs that Portia had been denied a child because he hadn't been able to give her one. Her heart strings had been mightily pulled except now, after only an hour and a half of the ongoing noise, inspection, chit chat and outright curiosity, she was ready to chuck in the towel and find the nearest exit.

This, even though she had been trying hard to find the whole thing exciting. James had ruefully told her that Andreas would not be attending, to which she had shrugged nonchalantly as though it mattered not in the slightest to her whether he attended or not. Then she had blown it by waspishly adding that he was probably way too busy living in the fast lane in London and probably sick to death of the countryside. To which James had countered, mildly, that her tone of bitterness was a little surprising, considering they seemed to have been getting along so brilliantly just before he left.

She began scouting around for her father. For someone who had made it his creed to avoid big parties at all costs, he seemed to be having a riotous time, catching up with old friends while holding court over all the local ones—including

Dot, who had kindly sprung into action and arranged the whole affair. Since they had numerous friends and acquaintances in common, most of whom she had diligently kept in touch with over the years, the guest list had been easily compiled and had run into several dozen. Over a hundred, in fact. She snatched at a passing tray, helping herself to another glass of champagne and a canapé, and heaved a small sigh of resignation as Toby Gilbert weaved his way towards her.

Would she ever have met a guy like Toby Gilbert if she hadn't entered this strange, elite world via the side door, being James Greystone's prodigal daughter? No. He was one of those men who would have existed on the fringes of her life, one of those successful, eligible lawyer-types who moved in a slightly different stratosphere to the one she had occupied. Suave, charming, well-dressed and undeniably posh.

He was just one of several who had come with older friends or relatives to 'brighten up the evening', as James had coyly put it. Only at the eleventh hour, when Elizabeth had already nervously donned her party gear and had been looking forward to the party with a deep sense of dread.

'You don't look as though you're having a ball.' His bright-blue eyes were amused and assessing as he helped himself from a passing tray to one of the intricate delicacies that must have taken some painstaking caterer ages to concoct. 'Can't say I blame you,' he continued drily. 'Must be hellish being held up for inspection and knowing that you're obliged to enjoy the experience.' His thick, blond hair was artfully cut, a little long at the front, but not so long that he wouldn't be taken seriously in his job. He was, she had to admit, the kind of man who would have no trouble with the women. It was woefully unfair that her head was so cluttered up with the wrong guy that she couldn't do more than return a wan smile and force herself to make polite small-talk.

She had promised herself not to think about Andreas. It seemed a vital step in weaning herself off him. She was sure she could do it. To aid the process, she swallowed the remainder of her champagne in one gulp, and was discomfited by the sensation of bubbles fizzing down the back of her throat.

Then she proceeded to listen politely, her head cocked to one side to demonstrate interest, even though her rebellious mind had broken free of its rein and was beginning to wander down all those forbidden routes. Which was why the sight of Andreas, leaning against the doorframe of the vast, crowded drawing-room and looking at her, was not at all disconcerting; she knew that it was just her crazy imagination playing tricks on her. She blinked to clear the picture and then gasped softly when she realised that the person now turning to address a few words to the fan club of tittering women who had circled him with interest was no figment of her imagination.

An imaginary Andreas would not now be laughing and flirting with the gaggle of blondes around him but then her imagination was a far cry from the reality, which was that Andreas had proved himself to be a guy who would happily seduce one woman while having another stashed away somewhere else. He was a guy who could still find it possible to think the worst of her even when he should have known better, should have seen that side of her that would never, ever take advantage of anyone. He was a man who had not been at all interested in what she had had to say. He was someone who could make a girl fall in love with him even though she didn't want to, and then turn around and treat her as though what they had briefly shared was meaningless.

She could feel a great ache of sadness and self pity well up inside her, and she refocused all her attention on the man in front of her, who suddenly seemed so hollow and insubstantial compared to the cad by the door—now holding a drink in his hand, although he had yet to take a sip of it.

Her nerves were suddenly stretched to screaming point as she forced herself to focus on Toby, to take an interest in what he was saying, reminding herself that he was a great guy whose attention was flattering and ego-boosting, and a soothing balm to her battered sense of self-worth.

But her skin felt hot and prickly, and out of the corner of her eye she was aware that Andreas had shaken off the gaggle of women. Like royalty, he couldn't move without someone wanting to shake his hand. By golly—she didn't want to admit it—but he looked drop-dead gorgeous. His black hair was swept away from his lean, darkly handsome face and his white shirt and black tailored tuxedo clung to him with loving perfection.

She wondered whether he had spotted her, and rather thought that if he had he would do his utmost to avoid her. He had made it clear in no uncertain terms that she disgusted him but, that aside, she was relieved that he had shown up. James had taken his refusal to attend the party on the chin, but he would have been hurting inside.

She was aware that she was making all the right noises. Who knew? Under normal circumstances, she might very well have been riveted by Toby's amusing account of a legal case he had handled a few months previously. Under normal circumstances, she might very well have been hanging on to hear the punchline to his anecdote. Sadly, she couldn't remember the last time she had experienced the luxury of normal circumstances, and they sure weren't normal now. Her nerves were all over the place and she was aware of every small movement of her body even though she now had her back to Andreas.

'Gilbert.'

The low, lazy drawl feathered the back of her neck and she felt her skin prickle as she slowly turned around. She imagined Andreas had targeted her not because he was dying to have a conversation with her, but probably because a week away had provided him with yet more fodder for attack.

'I haven't seen you around these parts recently. Still clinging to that job of yours at Taylor Merchants? I heard the pavements outside their offices are littered with unemployed lawyers, scrabbling around and wondering how they're going to survive without their bonuses. Hell, still—there's always money to be found in unexpected quarters. Wouldn't you agree, Elizabeth?' Andreas knew that it was a low blow, uncalled for. But he had never liked Toby Gilbert, and seeing the man involved in some kind of bonding conversation with Elizabeth had set his teeth more on edge. His teeth had already been set on edge the minute he had spotted her get-up. She was dressed to kill, and with enough potential victims to fill her little black book. James hadn't been kidding with that snide remark about wanting her to find a nice young man. The faint aroma of some very subtle perfume made his nostrils flare, but he was resisting the urge to look at her.

Toby had stiffened, but the respect and fear that Andreas was capable of instilling was powerful enough to elicit a polite reply to the obvious insult.

'Still hanging on, old man. And, as for money in unexpected places? Not the sort to chase a moneyed woman, although with or without James Elizabeth would make most heads turn…'

'Is that a fact?' The tightness in his chest was back, accompanied by a cyclonic rage that Andreas fought to contain.

The deadly softness of his voice made the hairs rise on the back of Elizabeth's neck. It also yanked her out of her trance-like state of absorption and catapulted her back into fighting spirit. She remembered that this was the man who had stolen her heart and returned the favour by treating her like something the cat had brought in, something unsavoury that he would have shoved instantly into the rubbish bin had his godfather not prevented it. Not content with that, now his casual, insolent insult penetrated her like a curare-tipped arrow. What more evidence did she need, to know that there was nothing left between them?

'Not everyone is terrified of surprises, Andreas—and, Toby, thank you for that compliment. It means a lot to me.' Elizabeth placed her hand gently on Toby's arm and shot Andreas a rebellious look from under her lashes. Just looking at the harsh, beautiful lines of his face was enough to make her feel giddy and, lord, how she hated that.

Andreas looked at her hand on Toby's arm and bolted down his drink in one gulp. 'Be a good chap,' he said pleasantly enough to Toby, even though the image of her hand on his arm was burning a hole in his head, 'and give us a few minutes. There's some stuff we need to discuss. Matters of estate.'

Toby's departure seemed to lock them into an intimate situation in which they were isolated from everyone around them. It was as if everything became background noise and motion, so great was the power Andreas could exert over her. She made a feeble attempt to break the spell by glancing around for help in the shape of her father, who was nowhere to be seen. He had been transformed from virtual recluse to party animal, it would seem.

'I didn't think you would be coming,' she said tightly, eyes returning to the man standing in front of her. His fabulous dark eyes were shuttered as he looked down at her; he gently swirled his empty glass in one hand, the other hand in his trouser pocket. He made every man in the room pale in comparison and that angered her, because his very presence seemed mockingly to undermine her efforts to get over him. James had very kindly made sure that there were people there her age just in case she got bored, she assumed—but all his efforts had been in vain because it just took one man to walk through the door and her disobedient eyes could see no one else. Even when he had been unbelievably rude. It wasn't fair!

'Nor did I, but in the end I couldn't resist the temptation to see how you were dealing with your new-found celebrity status.'

'I haven't got a new-found celebrity status.'

'By which I take it that you haven't been devouring any of the tabloids?'

'What?'

'My secretary kindly brought me a couple yesterday. You're not front-page news, but you do warrant a few paragraphs somewhere in the centre.'

The colour had drained away from Elizabeth's face as she imagined how that would look to Andreas. On the one hand she had been red in the face in her determination to prove to him how little James's wealth and status mattered, and on the other hand she had popped up in some wretched tabloid. Heaven only knew what they had had to say about her. James, she knew, would be indifferent, because he didn't care a jot for other people's opinions, and she was very glad that she had not come across any of the articles.

'There have been no reporters around here,' Elizabeth told him through gritted teeth, and he shrugged.

'James is not fodder for gossip. *Your* arrival on the scene is more a point of interest. And, I must say, you seem to have settled into your new role with…aplomb. You even…look different.' He reached out and curled his finger into some strands of her newly straightened hair, and Elizabeth froze as her body responded with slamming intensity. She pulled away.

'You mean less the unsophisticated bumpkin who showed

up here a couple of months ago?' She had a sudden vision of Amanda with her gorgeous, perfectly made-up face, her long, rangy model's body and her patina of gloss. 'I've straightened my hair and I'm wearing a designer dress because James insisted, but I'm the same person underneath. If you're looking for polish and real glamour, then there are quite a few of those types milling around. Or maybe you brought another one of your own with you?' She scanned the room, but it was impossible to tell because most of the guests were unfamiliar to her.

'So, I'm curious—how does all this now equate with your wish to find a simple job in the town? If I remember correctly, that *was* your intention?'

'You still want to believe the worst of me, don't you?'

'I'm interested to find out whether the simple life is still part of your package, or whether you've dumped that along with the fake persona and the persuasive bedside-manner.'

'I don't have to stand here listening to this!' But the sea of faces was uninviting and, besides, like a moth drawn to a flame, she found that she was unwilling to tear herself away from him. Indeed, against her will, she was aware of his height and his size with senses that were agonisingly over-sensitised. If she reached out she could touch him, and she clenched her hands into fists because the temptation was so frighteningly powerful. A terrible 'what if?' scenario presented itself in her feverish mind and she had to take a deep breath to steady herself. It was important to remember that this man had used and discarded her and was still, even now, happy to continue insulting her.

'How much of this was planned in advance?' Andreas knew that this was a conversation destined to go nowhere. However, he had been shaken up by James's intention on playing match-maker—and even more shaken up to find said plan already on the road to success, judging from the 'come and get me' outfit Elizabeth was wearing, and the obvious effect it was having on the unattached male guests. Gilbert couldn't have made his interest in Elizabeth more obvious if he had printed it on a sandwich board. Any casual assumption that she wouldn't be tempted by chinless wonders had bitten the dust with supersonic force.

His imagination now dive-bombed to a scenario in which she had suggested the match-making—the prodigal daughter working her sexiness in her search for the perfect mate. And sexy she damn well looked. Andreas felt himself stirring in his trousers so that he had to incline his body to one side, or in a second there was the very real possibility that the tell-tale bulge would become unmissable.

'Planned in advance?'

'Well, we know that the "getting to know you" approach worked like a dream—but were you also on board for the "meet the eligible bachelor" mission as well? Was that there in the planning stage from the very beginning? How long before walking down the aisle concludes the process?'

'Who knows?' Elizabeth, threw back at him recklessly, stung to the quick.

'So you don't deny that you had a game plan from the beginning?' Despite himself, Andreas was outraged at that level of deception.

'Why should I? It's not as if you believe a word I say anyway.'

This was not what Andreas wanted to hear, and he cursed himself for angling the conversation down the one-way street. 'So is Gilbert the guy you've lined up as Suitable Bachelor Number One?'

'Why does it matter to you one way or another?' Elizabeth gave a toss of her head, which felt like a very empowering thing to do at that moment in time. 'Maybe I'll have a few on the go at the same time. All's fair in love and war, as they say. And don't tell me that you disapprove, because you can't have one set of rules for yourself and another set for the rest of the world.'

'I don't believe I'm hearing this. And I take it you're harking back to those pointless remarks about Amanda?'

'I didn't think it was *pointless* to ask for an explanation as to how you could string both of us along at the same time!'

Born from the habit of a lifetime, Andreas answered swiftly and smoothly, 'I answer to no one.'

'Because you don't care about anyone but yourself,' Elizabeth muttered painfully. Her legs were finally beginning to function again, as was her cotton-wool brain. It was telling her that it was high time she made her escape, because too long in Andreas's presence did crazy things to her brain and she was terrified that under the defiant exterior he would glimpse the reality of how she felt about him.

'And Gilbert—I mean, *Toby*—is great. Good-looking, pleasant, smart…'

'Are you listing his attributes to remind yourself of them?' Andreas was finding it difficult to credit that he was levelling insults about a guy to whose existence he was utterly indifferent. Where the hell had his legendary cool gone? Green eyes met his squarely and he grimly reined in his impulse to continue their counter-productive argument. Whatever the hell the woman wanted to do was entirely her concern. He should wash his hands of her and walk away. Fortunately for the both of them, he thought, his mind finding ground with which he was comfortable and thereby restoring his equilibrium, he could see outside the box.

'But that's not what I wanted to talk to you about.'

Elizabeth watched him warily. They were standing on the sidelines, which didn't mean that there weren't frequent curious glances being thrown their way. 'People are looking at us. They're probably wondering what's going on.' If she had imagined that that might have put Andreas off his stride, she was sorely mistaken; he shrugged one elegant shoulder in a gesture of bored indifference.

'I have no problem with that.'

'Well, what did you want to talk to me about?'

'Now that you're a permanent part of my godfather's life, it's going to be a little tedious if you are antagonistic every time we meet, because meet we will. It's an inevitability.'

Elizabeth opened her mouth to protest that their antagonism was mutual, but closed it again, because that would have kick-started another round of battle for which she would doubtless be made to take the blame. The more she sniped, the faster he would realise how much he got under her skin, and she wanted to protect herself from that, so she drew herself up and nodded curtly.

'I am, and will continue to be, devoted to my godfather and as such I will visit as often as I always have. If you think that I used you as a bit of entertainment, because my main squeeze was in London and out of reach, then that's your business, but you've got to get over it.' Back in control, Andreas felt the ratcheted tension inside him begin to subside. With ruthless efficiency, he cleared his mind of the disturbing images of Elizabeth with Gilbert. Dwelling on that was definitely not a good idea. Dark, veiled eyes swept over her without a noticeable change of expression. 'But, like it or not, we shared something and because of that I'm going to give you a bit of advice.'

'I don't need your advice.' *But, like it or not, we shared something…* Was that how he summarised a relationship that had torn apart her foundations and changed her from the inside out?

'You do need my advice,' Andreas intoned drily, pleased

that he was big enough to look out for her interests even though she had turned out to be, if not a cheat, then certainly a pretty accomplished liar. Never mind the semantics; that subject was still up for debate. 'Because you might be dressed in scarlet but you're still green behind the ears.'

She half-opened her mouth and he held up an imperious hand. 'You'll thank me for this,' he informed her, 'but no thanks needed. My godfather is overjoyed at his prodigal daughter turning up out of the blue, and out of love and respect I am obliged to put any concerns of mine to bed. I am also morally obliged to warn you that if you plan on setting your sights on any of the men in this room then you would be wise to give it some thought.'

'Because I'm not really in their class?'

Andreas gave a short, mocking laugh and raised his eyebrows in wry amusement. 'The world's come a long way from those upstairs-downstairs days,' he drawled. 'Sure, there are a few left who cling to their landed-gentry status, and nightly pray that it won't be invaded by riff raff, but you'd be surprised how a shrinking economy can do away with false pride. No; you should give it some serious thought because they enjoy having playthings—even Gilbert, that great, good-looking, pleasant, smart guy. From what I've seen in you, you aren't prepared to take on the no-strings-attached-plaything role.'

'Are you talking about us?'

'I'm giving you some good advice.'

'I wasn't ever going to move to London, because I wanted to be *here*...close to James. I didn't know that everything would come out in the open the way it did.'

'And, taking James out of the equation, you would have been ready and willing to take on the role of plaything?' Andreas was driven to ask the question, but even as it left his mouth he regretted the impulse. What was it about this woman? No sooner had he put his wayward emotions under lock and key than he discovered that the bolts had been shot and careless, random thoughts were sneaking in uninvited.

The sudden blush that spread across her cheeks, and the taut silence that greeted this question, was answer enough. Realisation dawned on Andreas with sudden, blinding clarity.

'You don't *do* plaything, do you?' he said slowly, his bitter-chocolate eyes lingering on her evident embarrassment. 'And, when I asked you to move in with me, you would still have turned me down flat even if James had not been a deciding factor because you wanted more than just sharing my bed and my space.'

'I—I don't know what you're talking about.' But she stumbled over her words and then cleared her throat assertively. 'And I really think that it's time for me to mingle. Like you said, this party is all about my father introducing me to his friends, bringing me into his life and making sure that everyone knows it, even if some might disapprove. Like you.'

'Nice try.'

Elizabeth stared at him mutely. Everything about him oozed self-confidence, and right now more than self-confidence. A certain knowledge that had her cringing inwardly.

'What were you hoping for?'

'I wasn't hoping for anything!' To her own ears, she could hear the undercurrent of desperation.

'Would a more substantial offer have done the job? Did you want a marriage proposal? A ring on that finger? Did you think that I would fit the role of suitable husband? You must have been disappointed. I'm man enough to admit that sex with you was…what can I say?…in a league of its own. But marriage…'

'I wouldn't marry you if you were the last person on the face of the earth!' Elizabeth told him in a fierce undertone. 'But you're right when you say that I'm looking for more out of life than just a romp in the hay and a wave goodbye when it's over and done with.'

'And you think your chances are good with Gilbert? London's a village. I personally know four of his past conquests.'

Elizabeth wished that she could wipe that curling smirk from his beautiful mouth.

'Thank you for that. I'll take my chances. And, just to tell you, I think that I've learnt a lot from you and the most important thing I've learnt is that arrogant men who think they don't owe anyone anything at all are the kind of men I should steer clear of!' She spotted Toby across the room and gave him an insouciant wave.

'Toby might be *just* the tonic I need! Because you're right: in this day and age, who the heck gets involved for the sole purpose of sticking on a wedding ring and walking up the aisle? So, thank you for your advice. You've done me a big favour, because I see now that what I really need is just a bit of fun. With someone who doesn't think that he's the greatest catch in the world, and won't have girlfriends chasing me across the country so that they can get their own back!'

CHAPTER NINE

ELIZABETH'S compelling and assertive exit was somewhat tarnished by her slight stumble as she spun around, and she reminded herself to never wear high heels again. Having sung Toby's praises to the sky, she now felt duty-bound to seek him out. He was outside, sitting on one of the garden benches, smoking.

'I know, I know. I should give it up.' He looked at her and grinned. 'Finished your *tête à tête* with the wonder boy? He didn't seem to be in the most jolly of moods, but, then again, when has Andreas ever been in a jolly mood? He's never been noted for his ability to see the lighter side of life.'

Elizabeth opened her mouth to rush to immediate defence of him, but then stopped herself, because defending Andreas just wasn't going to do. The more she fixated on all the great things about him, the things that she had kidded herself she had been privileged to see, the deeper she would fall into the trap of never being able to let him go. If there was one thing tonight had shown her, it was the necessity of letting him go.

When Toby patted the space beside him, she hesitantly sat down, and, when she laughed about being cold and he proffered his jacket, she tentatively accepted it. If step one in getting over Andreas was to ditch the compulsion to compare every single man to him and find them all wanting, then step two was surely to accept that she would need an open mind when it came to other men. No, she certainly wasn't going to leap into bed with someone else when she was still raw and bleeding from a broken heart, but she wasn't going to go into perpetual hibernation either. Toby might not be the man of her dreams, and it might take her weeks, months or even years to find the man of her dreams, but find him she would.

She was hardly aware of them walking back towards the house, Toby's arm slung heavily over her shoulder, although every muscle in her body went into full-alert mode as she spotted Andreas across the drawing room, his hair lightly tousled from the breeze blowing through the open French doors.

He was busily talking to James, his dark eyes lazy and arresting. He sensed her entrance even before he saw her, and there was a brief, disconcerting few seconds when his mind seemed to literally develop a peculiar kind of rigor mortis as he took in the unpleasant sight of Gilbert draped all over her like a rash. He had come to this party expecting vapid pretty-boys, the kind of airheads who would not have interested her in a million years. He was cottoning on pretty fast to the sickening fact that she might just be crazy enough to consider them as potential love-interests. Or one in particular, at any rate.

Half of him protested immediate indifference to the fact, because he was a man in ultimate control of his life. He always had been and nothing there would be allowed to change. The other half, however, was thrown into crazy confusion, and he fought against this half with an instinct that had its roots in self-preservation. He was not even aware of the struggle inside him as he watched her flush to the roots of her hair, as she said something low and soft to Gilbert, before reluctantly making her way over to where they were standing.

Feeling the steady, inscrutable gaze of Andreas's eyes on

her burning face, Elizabeth resolutely turned to James and began an earnest conversation about the party, which enabled her to more or less exclude Andreas from the picture. Most normal people would have taken the hint, she thought, but naturally he remained where he was. She didn't have to see his face to know that there would be a sardonic grin curving his mouth as he took little sips of wine and continued to ruminate on the hilarity of a woman in search of some replacement therapy.

People were beginning to show more interest in the food; an extensive buffet replaced the intricate finger-foods that had done the rounds. Elizabeth gave James a peck on the cheek, turning her back on Andreas with relief.

She was doing a good job of pretending that he was nowhere around when she felt a tap on her shoulder just as she was about to move away from the buffet table with her plate of food.

There was no need for her to turn around to guess the identity of the person invading her space. There was only one person she knew who had zero qualms about invading her space.

'Tut, tut,' Andreas said, having captured her attention. 'Shouldn't you be with your target audience? Leave him for too long and you might find his attention beginning to stray.' He was grimly aware that he was in serious danger of behaving like a loser—how else would you describe a guy who couldn't leave a woman alone? Even when his head was telling him that it was the only thing to do. Confusion had taken up residence somewhere deep inside him and he didn't know what the hell to do with it because it was something he had never felt before.

Elizabeth bracingly told herself that she would not, absolutely would *not,* allow Andreas to get under her skin. The second he did that, she was back on the merciless treadmill, see-sawing emotions, grinding misery and self-pity. This party would be her opportunity to launch herself into a different place.

'He's not my *target audience,*' she said. 'And, anyway, it's a downright insult to imply that the only way I can get a guy to be interested in me is if I lock him in a room and throw away the key.'

Andreas had a disconcerting thought about the satisfaction he would get in locking *her* in a room and throwing away the key. He stamped down such an irrational notion with a dark scowl. He would not permit himself to ask her whether she intended to date Gilbert.

'Anyway, I should be mingling. James won't think I'm enjoying myself unless I do.' She gave him a long, cool look and headed away to one of the tables which had been set up in a massive marquee that adjoined the set of French doors out to the garden. The dining-room table had been reserved for the contingent of older guests because it was altogether more comfortable. Which meant that for the next hour at least she would have to make continuing conversation with the young people, who were pleasant enough, in fact more pleasant than she might have expected, but with whom she essentially had nothing in common. If she could only take her own good advice to heart, she would give Toby the green light he was clearly looking for, but she dispiritedly realised that amber was the best she could offer, and even that was a reluctant concession.

Out of the corner of her eye, she spotted Andreas as he cast his hawk-like gaze across the marquee, finally settling on her. Suddenly the plate of food in front of her lost its appeal as he made his way towards the place she had taken up at the very back of the marquee, a solitary figure in red, content to observe. She would mingle in a minute.

'I have come to apologise,' were his opening words as he settled himself next to her and began to tuck into his food.

That wasn't what Elizabeth had expected, and after a few seconds of bewilderment she, too, began eating. With only the minimum of notice, Dot had managed to oversee some splendid catering; although Elizabeth could feel herself stiff with tension, she could appreciate the delicate, flaky texture of the salmon and the crispness of the salad. Less welcome was that stirring of her senses which always happened whenever Andreas was in the vicinity, even when he was in full-attack mode.

The tables were groaning under the weight of bottles of wine, and he poured them both a glass of white. People coming in saw them and discreetly moved to other tables.

'You're scaring off the guests,' Elizabeth muttered. She was determined to let him know that his presence was the last thing she wanted, but her body was singing a different song. Just the mesmerising sight of his long fingers as he tore his bread, and the way his dark hair curled around the silver, metal band of his watch, made her tummy do cartwheels.

'Good. I hate apologising in front of an audience.'

'When have you ever done that?'

'You're right. Never. And now is definitely not the time to break that record.'

Elizabeth made a concentrated effort to try and relax. If she could focus on all the things about him that made her mad, then she might actually be able to curtail her wildly inappropriate responses to him. But of course that was all well and good in theory. In practice, her mouth was dry, her pulses were racing and there was a tell-tale tingling in her breasts that spoke shameless volumes.

'I admit I may have been a little out of order to imply that you were jumping on a bandwagon with this sudden array of possible suitors.' He refused to narrow that down to Gilbert.

'Possible suitors? That's a ridiculous idea! James just thought that it might be nice to meet some young people, and the only young people he knows are related to older people he knows. Or else are friends of friends.' She thought maybe she should imply here that Toby was a serious contender, that she was interested in him. Wouldn't it prove to Andreas that she was on the way to getting over him as easily as he had got over her? Stringing the thought together, though, was a Herculean feat when his proximity was turning her brain to mush, and that softly worded apology had sent her pulses racing.

Andreas thought it better to keep to himself that James had had much more in mind than altruism when he had compiled his guest list, but he made a mental note to have a quiet word with his godfather about the foolishness of trying to play matchmaker. He considered that the very least he could do, as the gentleman he undoubtedly was. And she hadn't mentioned Gilbert, which was a good thing. Clinging to that omission was less of a good thing, but Andreas didn't dwell on that.

'Well, whatever.' He gave an elegant shrug, pushed his plate to one side and angled his chair so that he was facing her directly. His ability to devote one-hundred percent of his attention on the person to whom he was speaking was part of the essence of his charm, but right now it made Elizabeth feel a little giddy and confused.

'The fact is that I believed the worst of you, and for that I owe you an apology.' She had stopped eating so that she could stare at him with bated breath, and he now took her fingers in his hand and idly played with them.

Elizabeth felt as though there had been a sudden drop in the oxygen levels. She literally froze and then, when her lungs began working again, told herself that this was an absent-minded and casual gesture from a man who had moved on and so could do this, could touch her without getting into knots about it. As she was doing.

Andreas could feel the tension in her body as clearly as if it had announced itself in bright, neon lettering across her forehead and that in itself was strangely pleasing. As was the feel of her slender, smooth fingers between his. He found that he had a very clear memory of the feel of her, soft, satin-smooth, wholly and utterly feminine. It must have lodged somewhere at the back of his mind, or maybe it had been absorbed into his bloodstream, because along with that memory came an overwhelming urge to recapture the completeness of being with her. He didn't just want to hold her hand in a caring, friendly way. He wanted to lead her hand to his body so that she could touch him where it was now beginning to physically hurt. He wanted his hand to dip into the sweet moistness of her. He wanted to watch her face as she moved against his fingers, and see her eyelids flutter as she located that special place and began grinding sinuously, exciting herself, and luxuriating in the knowledge that her excitement was his excitement. He had taught her to do that, to feel comfortable with her body, and comfortable with his vocal and visual appreciation of it.

Like a possessive master selfishly holding on to his star pupil, Andreas gritted his teeth in the face of the glaring reality that he just wasn't ready, willing or even *able* to let her go. He was in the grip of a desire much stronger than anything he had known before. Why else had he come to this party? He had plenty to do in London. He had been away from his office for a considerable length of time. James had not been at all disconcerted by his refusal, and yet he had found himself coming anyway. Why? Because he wasn't ready to let her go.

It irked him that she could still get to him even though she had affronted him on pretty much every level. She had contrived to keep secrets from him, even when they had become lovers. She had reacted to Amanda's appearance on the scene by hurling unjust accusations at him, and he hadn't explained himself. It wasn't his style. Yet she had been less than impressed by his boundaries, choosing to behave in a fashion which he would have found unacceptable in any other woman. Most gallingly of all, she had turned down his offer that she become his mistress. That had been a direct hit to his sense of pride and to his ego.

Taking all those things into account, Andreas knew that he should have had no problem whatsoever in walking away from her. In fact—in theory, at least—he should have had no problem walking away from her and straight into the arms of someone else, someone fashioned from that mould to which he had become accustomed; one of those women who didn't keep him up at night, never questioned his authority and was inordinately pleased with whatever shows of generosity he chose to display. Isobel should have fitted that bill, but he hadn't been remotely turned on by her, and she had ceased to exist the minute their date had come to its abrupt conclusion.

James's confession that he wanted Elizabeth to find stability with a boyfriend, and to that end was going to invite some eligible chaps, should have caused resounding cynicism and a sigh of relief that he was rid of her. Instead, he had ruminated all the way to his helicopter, his formidable, hard-headed logic and ferocious self-control for once taking a back seat behind other emotions which he had no inclination to analyse.

It all went to prove conclusively to him that lust was something he had previously underrated. All that ugly confusion and tightness in his chest was testimony to the power of unfinished business.

He released her hand and sat back, content in the knowledge that her body still stirred for him. She still quivered in his presence, and it would seem responded to him exactly like he responded to her, if only she was aware of the fact.

He was acutely attuned to her every small movement, from the nervous fidgeting of her fingers to the delicate, heightened colour staining her cheeks.

'I won't deny that I was angry when I discovered that you'd taken us in.'

'I explained.'

'You did. And there's no need to retrace old ground. You did what you felt you had to do, and I can see that you reached a certain point when backtracking might have been a little daunting.' Andreas discovered that he actually did believe that. He suspected that he had believed her from the start, although his ingrained inclination towards suspicion, which had always stood him in good stead, had compelled him to question her motives.

Elizabeth breathed a little sigh of relief and half-closed her eyes. 'It means a lot to hear you say that,' she confessed, her eyes widening as she looked at him and began drowning in the steady intensity of his gaze.

She wondered if he would touch her again, and when she realised that she was longing for it she resolutely stuck her hands under her thighs. Just in case they started wandering of their own accord. It would have taken a lot for him to say what he had said, because he was nothing if not supremely arrogant, but say it he had.

'I wouldn't want you to feel uncomfortable in my presence,' Andreas murmured softly. As his glittering, black eyes collided with hers, Elizabeth drew her breath in, feeling very much as if she had stepped out from the pages of a Victorian novel and was on the verge of swooning. She resisted the manic temptation to giggle when she wondered whether the generously supplied tables also had a line in smelling salts. She wondered what he would do if she told him that his fraternal reassurance was the last thing she wanted.

'I don't,' she said with equal composure, even though her heart was hammering madly in her chest. 'And I'm really glad that you believe me. I know I've said this before, but I wasn't going to say anything about…well, about anything, if your girlfriend…'

'*Ex*-girlfriend. And, by the way, we had broken up before I started sleeping with you.' His eyes roved lazily across her flushed face. Yielding on this one small matter was worth it to see the shell-pink blush that spread across her cheeks.

'Why didn't you say so at the time?'

'I am not in the habit of explaining myself.' He gave a theatrical shrug of his broad shoulders and shot her a smile that literally brought her out in beads of perspiration. 'But in this instance I feel it's justified, so that I clear the air between us. I wouldn't want you labouring under the misconception that I'm the kind of guy who would ever sleep with more than one woman at the same time. For me, making love is not to be taken lightly.' His voice dropped a notch to a husky, sexy drawl. 'Nor, while I am being totally honest, would I want you to think that you were anything but bloody amazing. There are times when I close my eyes and I can still taste you on my tongue.'

He sat back, leaving her with that thought, which affected him like a shot of adrenaline, and looked around at the marquee which was filling out nicely with people.

'But never mind that. You probably don't want to hear that, especially not now, when you should be enjoying yourself with all the guys James has invited here for your benefit.' He still couldn't bring himself to single Gilbert out by name but he was damn sure that the guy was not even on the fringes of her consciousness as she breathlessly watched him.

Elizabeth, taking her cue from him, tried to clear her head of the devastating memory of them making love.

'*Are* you enjoying yourself, by the way?'

She nodded, and then when she had located her voice said evenly, 'It's a bit over the top, but it was a kind thought, and I think James is thrilled to have all his old friends around him.'

'I don't suppose you've ever had a lavish do like this before?' There was nothing snide in his observation and she allowed herself to relax a little. She found herself telling him about the parties she had had as a child growing up, and about how hard her mother had tried to compensate for the lack of a father. She knew she was babbling, because she was nervous and over-aware of him sitting there with his head inclined to one side, for all the world as though he really cared about what she was saying. But she was proud of herself that she could communicate like this, when her head was swimming and her body felt as though it was submerged in treacle. That said something, didn't it?

People were beginning to drift over towards them, plates in hands, while waiters scuttled around topping up glasses, making sure that wine was poured at the tables.

In under a minute, their table would be full, and the tedious business of mingling would begin. It was a shame. Having swotted away the irritating business of potential suitors, having confronted the unexpected fact that he still fancied the hell out of her—never mind that she had rejected him, a little technicality that should have killed off all remnants of lust stone-dead—Andreas was enjoying the idea of showing her just how little Gilbert, or anyone else for that matter, meant to her. Of getting her back into bed. With him. Where she belonged. Until such time as his crazy desire fizzled out, which it inevitably would.

No. Until such time as *their* crazy, *mutual* desire fizzled out. Because his antennae had honed in on her responses to him and relayed back to his brain that he certainly wasn't the only one who thought that there was unfinished business between them.

But there was no rush, was there? A feeling of warm contentment spread through him, blessed relief after the puzzling array of frustrated emotions that had been swirling through him like toxins over the past week. The uncertainty that had gripped him when he had seen her mingling with other guys was subsiding.

He didn't want to be in the grip of those weird, conflicting emotions and he therefore reduced the situation to its basic essentials: she still wanted him, he still wanted her. And, most importantly, they had been lovers. In that respect, he held the trump card. He noted that Toby was nowhere in evidence, and that gave him a further feeling of having landed on safe ground. He wondered whether she was already regretting her haste in turning down his magnanimous offer for her to accompany him to London. He hoped so. Was she silently making comparisons, drawing obvious conclusions? Was she realising that, when it came to giving herself, *he* was the only contender? It shocked him to realise how much he desired that outcome.

In a life previously fuelled by the demands of work, women had been ready and willing at the click of a finger. He therefore had never had the need to indulge in anticipation. Since when had anticipation ever been necessary when the conclusions were all foregone?

He was anticipating now, and the anticipation was sweet after that previous, sickening assault on his equilibrium at seeing her turn her attentions to someone else.

He was even enjoying watching her as, meal over, she immediately left the table so that she could dutifully enjoy herself. She hadn't been brought up in this sort of society—would have probably baulked at mixing with a bunch of mostly toffee-nosed people a few months ago—but she had grown in confidence since then. He remained where he was, sprawled in his chair at the table. Having demonstrated such an outstanding lack of enthusiasm for the various women who had optimistically sidled across to him to 'renew their acquaintance', he had eventually been left in peace. Lazily he looked on as Elizabeth chatted and mixed, and only glanced at her watch a couple of times when she thought no one was looking.

In fact, he only snapped out of his watchful reverie when his godfather approached him, with Dot protectively hanging on to him, even though his opening words to Andreas were, 'Woman can't leave me alone! Thinks I need propping up just in case I collapse in the middle of my own damn party!'

Andreas noticed with amusement that he didn't seem intent on shrugging off the protective hold, despite his grumbling, and for a while he allowed himself to be distracted by his godfather. It was getting late. People were stopping by to relay their thanks, amidst much warm words about dropping by for visits. Most had brought drivers, some had ordered taxis, and none, thankfully, were staying over. Dot had suggested that it might not be a good idea, given the fact that James would be exhausted the following day and would not be able to face another round of entertaining.

By a little after one, James was safely tucked up for the night, tired but still on high from the success of his impromptu gathering; the house was as good as empty. Only a handful of cleaning staff remained in the kitchen tidying away dishes or else scouring the house for stray glasses and crockery.

Andreas could have relayed back Elizabeth's movements down to the last second, due to a watchfulness that was extraordinary for him. He knew who she had spoken to and for how long. Had noted her body language when she had been with the Gilbert creep, and had been pleased that all those miniscule signals that indicated interest were stupendously absent, at least on her part. He also knew what time Gilbert had departed, and had observed with satisfaction that the goodbyes had been a general affair, not a cosy one-to-one business. He also knew that she was making herself useful, bringing in glasses that had been left outside; she would never be the kind of person who took it for granted that other people were there to wait on her hand and foot. That was one of those little things that he liked about her.

He was waiting for her as she returned from her final trip to the kitchen with a trayful of champagne flutes, and as he blocked her path she could feel every nerve ending in her body ratchet up into screaming awareness.

He looked as fresh as a daisy, despite the missing tie, the shirt sleeves carelessly cuffed, the tousled hair. She, on the other hand, felt like Cinderella several hours after the witching hour.

'Join me for a drink?' Andreas noted her discomfort and was amused by it.

'You must be joking. It's nearly one-thirty in the morning!'

'I know. Shocking, isn't it?'

'It's been a long day,' she mumbled inadequately.

'And you're glad it's over.'

'Very glad.' Elaboration on this seemed to be required. 'I'm not used to all of this.' She gestured to the now-empty hall, and then self-consciously to her worse-for-wear dress.

'Have you considered that this might just be the start of James's quest to make sure that you're happy and entertained? You'll have to become accustomed to the Tobys and the Ruperts and the Alexanders…' The bundling of random names neatly downplayed the significance of any one in particular.

Elizabeth's eyes glazed over. 'I think they only came here out of curiosity,' she blurted out, alarmed at the prospect of having more well-connected, eligible men wheeled out in front of her. James was well intentioned but misguided.

'You have become something of a catch,' Andreas remarked wryly. 'Surely you're not so naive that you don't see that? The recession has barely skimmed the surface of James's fortune. Like it or not, if you want to have freedom of choice, you're going to have to spell it out in words of one syllable.'

'I don't need you to look out for me, thank you very much.' She was desperate to be away from his suffocating presence, but the mesmeric pull of his eyes glued her to the spot until her pink tongue darted out lightly to moisten her dry lips.

'Maybe I need to look out for my godfather's fortune,' Andreas answered distractedly. 'No one can move faster at demolishing an inheritance than an out-of-work banker who suddenly finds himself down on his luck. I want to make sure that you don't become a sucker for someone who knows how to spin a good tale.'

'Oh—either I need to lock a man up to keep him interested, or else I'm too stupid to differentiate between the minnows and the sharks! Thanks very much!' Insults, insults, insults—yet instead of fleeing her disobedient feet refused to budge.

'You're welcome.' In actual fact, he knew that she was nobody's pushover underneath that softly yielding exterior. But he was enjoying watching her face. He hadn't thought it was possible for a woman to get under his skin to the extent that this one had, which just went to show that life could still hold surprises.

'Anyway, there's no need for you to be concerned. I've already told James that I don't want anything from him. Not a penny. In fact, I'm going into town on Monday to have a look for a job. I've been chatting to a local guy, and he said that there are lots of vacant positions, especially if I'm not fussy about what I do. Even if I don't move out immediately,

I intend to do my fair share towards helping with the groceries and stuff like that.'

'That's incredibly noble, but I have a suspicion that James would hate that. Don't forget, you're the daughter he never knew he had. More than that, he loved you before he knew who you were. Course he's going to want to spoil you.'

Elizabeth hesitated, taken in by the seductive logic of what he was saying.

'He's also going to want to think that you're happy here. He wasn't born yesterday. He knows that for a young girl things can sometimes get a little...*challenging* around here. He will also be aware of the fact that you came here to suss him out, to get to know him; it was the reason you stayed. But, now that everything is out in the open, there just might be the fear that you'll start wanting to return to the big city.'

'And a parade of guys would keep me grounded?'

'These are country folk, even if they might bide their time in the big city,' Andreas pointed out. 'Their lives are inextricably tied up with their parents' estates, and their hearts and souls are never too far away from the country pile. Anyway.' He glanced away in a thoughtful fashion. 'It's entirely up to you what you do. You did mention that guys like Toby might be fun, especially after us...'

'I never said that I didn't have fun with you.' Elizabeth jumped in feverishly, then reddened at what she had blurted out.

'I'm glad to hear it.' Andreas allowed a heartbeat of silence to elapse. This strange little game of one step forward, two steps back was new to him, but he wasn't going to help her along the path of realising just how much she still yearned for him. He would wait for her to come to him and then he would have her, and he didn't think that she would be complaining.

'Because that wasn't the impression I got at the end.' He dangled the memory of the great sex they had had and left her to contemplate what she had thrown away. When she stared down at the ground, he had to resist the tremendous urge to sweep her bright hair away from her face and assuage his hunger on her full, half-parted mouth. It was frustrating that every time he thought he was in control of the situation, guiding it to the place where he wanted it to be—the place where it was *destined* to be—he seemed to lose his foothold. Tonight had heralded an onslaught of destabilising emotions and at the forefront of them was the certainty that he wanted her back. For good? No, surely not! He wasn't a 'for good' kind of guy…

'I just didn't want to move back to London.'

'Understood.' Andreas frowned. In the great scheme of things, dwelling on this particular sore point was not to his liking.

'Really?'

'Really.' His voice was dry and rueful. 'Which isn't to say that you didn't do lasting damage to my ego…' He gave a low, sexy laugh and leaned against the banister. He folded his arms and slanted that slow smile of his that could make any rational woman go weak at the knees. She had a blinding memory of how incredible it had been working alongside him, and then when they had become lovers enjoying a passion of which she had never considered herself capable. Like an ice sculpture subjected to the scorching intensity of white-heat, every pore in her being had melted at his touch.

Assailed by the power of memory and the reality of the man standing in front of her, Elizabeth was momentarily disabled, and she gripped the doorframe so fiercely that her knuckles turned white.

'I wouldn't overestimate my worth,' she said, making light of his remark, wondering whether there was a woman alive who could do any sort of damage, lasting or otherwise, to his ego.

'Why not? You might be surprised.'

Elizabeth felt her breath catch in her throat. This was heady stuff. She didn't need it. She just didn't have the right artillery to deal with the lazy caress of his words and the intimate huskiness of his voice. She could feel the pulse in her neck throbbing like a visible, uninvited sign of her excitement, and she wondered if he could see it too. There wasn't much he ever missed. She looked down, seeking divine inspiration from the ground, but her breathing was laboured as she looked back up and her eyes tangled with his.

She had no idea what malicious finger of fate made her lean towards him. She didn't mean to. In fact, she had fought very hard *not* to. But lean towards him she did, reaching out to curl her fingers around the collar of his shirt so that she could pull him towards her; like a drowning man tasting his first drop of life-giving water, she parted her mouth and kissed him with a desperate, greedy urgency that thrilled and sickened her at the same time.

She curved her treacherous body into his, pressing hard against him, and angling her legs so that his arousal could stimulate her aching wetness through the flimsy fabric of her dress.

Lord knew, but anyone could come upon them at any given moment. Much as Andreas was up for adventure when it came to sex, being caught in full *flagrante* in his godfather's house, like a randy teenager who couldn't make it up the stairs in time, was not his thing. Even so, with her body doing wickedly arousing things against him, he couldn't resist hitching up her dress so that he could plunge an exploratory finger into her moist wetness. He moved it, found that tender, swollen bud, pressed delicately until she gasped and shuddered and then very reluctantly withdrew his hand and straightened down her dress.

'Not here,' he said roughly, and just like that, in the space of two words, the moment was lost. Horrified, Elizabeth pulled away sharply as the consequences of her behaviour congealed in her head like a poisonous tumour. What was she doing? She had already succumbed to Andreas's persuasive charm and jettisoned all her principles in the process. She knew that he was a one-hundred percent, red-blooded alpha male who took what he wanted, enjoyed it for a while and then moved on. Okay, so maybe he was telling the truth and he had already dumped Amanda before he'd begun sleeping with her, but that didn't change the guy's basic moral guidelines. He didn't *do* love. He *did* sex. He didn't *do* commitment. He did fast-escape just as soon as his boredom levels were breached.

Furthermore, he had made a point of warning her off the guys at the party, and Toby in particular, and she could only think that he had done that because he hadn't been ready for her to walk away. As he had once told her, there was nothing he relished more than a challenge. To quarantine the competition and move in for the kill. And she had aided and abetted and opened the door to more hurt and pain by giving him the green light.

What did she need to get her house in order? She had ditched her pride for a couple of seconds of passion. The trade-off made her feel weakly sick, and she abruptly turned away from him.

'I can't do this,' she muttered, snatching her arm away when he tried to hold her. God, pathetic fool that she was, she was trembling like a leaf in a high wind.

'Stop pretending that you don't feel what I feel.'

'And stop asking me to pretend that it's all that I want.'

'I thought you wanted fun.'

'I just said that. I…' She looked at him steadily and drew in a deep breath. 'I want the whole nine yards. You know that. So hopping into bed with you isn't an option.'

'You mean it's not an option unless I offer you marriage.

Because not even cohabitation would work for you, would it? Well, let me tell you straight away, that's not on the cards and never will be.' Blackmailed into marriage? No way! Was any addiction worth that? Addictions, like everything else, could be overcome; he just wasn't used to having one. But no addiction would get the better of him. He was invulnerable, and if any little voice in his head dared to disagree then he would squash it.

But he couldn't look at her. He would walk away. Because no one took control away from him, even a witch with eyes the colour of sunlit sea, hair that shimmered like burnished gold and a smile that could screw with his head like nothing he had ever experienced before…

CHAPTER TEN

ELIZABETH pulled the comb through her long hair, leant towards the mirror on her dressing table and glared. She had done quite a bit of that over the past ten days. In response to James's relentless curiosity, she had finally confessed that she had had a bit of a minor *contretemps* with his godson—more a heated debate than a full-fledged argument, she had felt compelled to elaborate, with her fingers tightly crossed behind her back, and that Andreas was a louse. Beyond that she had not expanded, and in fact had managed to eventually steer the subject away by producing a replacement.

She had managed to find herself a job. It was only a temporary one, working at the local village school in the admin department, but she was hoping for an extension. That change of subject had had the desired effect of diverting James's needling questions and speculations, some of which had landed with disturbing accuracy. He had moved on to the less-fraught topic of what she intended to do long-term, and then to his familiar lament that she would find life dull and boring in Somerset. That she would leave just when they were getting to know one another, and would return to London to lead a wildly glamorous life from which he would be excluded. Now if she met a nice, young local chap… Then he had inserted slyly, 'Or there's always my godson. No woman calls a man a louse without good reason, but I'm certain you two could patch up your differences—and how comforting for me if you and Andreas…'

At that point, Elizabeth had made a radical decision. It was no good harbouring silly fantasies that Andreas would ever be anything more than he was capable of being. What they had had was conclusively over because their long-term wants and needs were a million miles apart. She didn't know if Andreas would ever settle down but she knew that when he did it certainly wouldn't be with her. With a brutality which he had probably found necessary, just in case she was driven to harbour any unrealistic expectations, he had spelled that out for her in words of one syllable.

It had been the most humiliating moment in her life. It had also provoked some soul-searching truths which she had forced herself to acknowledge. Truth one was that an extraordinary circus of events had thrown them together, but that without those extenuating circumstances nothing would ever have happened between them. Even if their paths had crossed, and even if she had stared at him the way every single woman on the face of the planet seemed to stare at him, he would never have returned the look; in normal conditions, she just wouldn't have been the type of woman to interest him. He wouldn't have bothered getting to know her, because men like Andreas didn't bother getting to know anyone who didn't immediately grab their attention with flamboyant good looks that matched their own. In every area of his life, he was the most complicated man she had ever met, but when it came to the opposite sex he was as shallow as a puddle.

He had ended up in bed with her because he had been isolated from his usual routine and because, in that isolation, he had come to see her as a novelty. Like a fool, she had not similarly seen *him* as a novelty. Like a complete idiot, she had embraced him as the real thing, and compromised her common sense which had been vocal in telling her that she was being stupid. And, just in case she started getting the wrong ideas, he had felt the need to state the obvious. It had been the final, stinging reminder of why she needed to move on.

Never mind moving on with any of the guys she had met at the party; Toby had telephoned her the day after and she had been polite but evasive, and he had taken the hint. The truth was that she was still the same girl she had always been, and high fliers from a different walk of life were never going to be the sort of men she would find lifetime happiness with.

Hence her conflicted emotions as she stared at her disgruntled face in the mirror. She would braid her hair. It wasn't the sexiest look on the face of the earth, but then she wasn't sexy; forget how Andreas had once made her once feel. Nor was she looking for someone who wanted to get her into bed to pass the time of day—or night, for that matter. She was looking for kindness, consideration, a man who didn't resent a few months of chaste kisses while they got to know one another.

Whether Tom Lloyd, one of the visiting teachers with whom she had been persuaded to have a cup of coffee, fitted the bill she had no idea. But he was young, affable and didn't threaten. He had been forward enough to approach her as he had spotted her leaving after her interview, but not so forward that he had jumped in with a dinner invitation. That said something. He had asked her about herself, and had been interested but not over-impressed at her recent family connections. Another tick for him. In fact, they had chatted for over an hour, and now they were meeting for lunch.

It would be nice, Elizabeth thought despairingly. And what choice did she have? Retreating from the world so that she could nurse her wounds would make her even more vulnerable than she already was. After Andreas, Tom might prove just the calming tonic she needed, even if James had seen fit to disagree volubly.

'Sounds a namby-pamby to me!' he had barked, before she had even finished talking. The fact that Tom was reasonably local was a trump card that had been waved aside like an irritating wasp. However local he was, nothing had saved him from being 'wishy washy', 'dull as dishwater', 'boring, and probably with a sackful of hang-ups and issues' and what the hell damn woman would want to get involved with someone who needed sorting out, especially his daughter?

Worse than all that, he had asked her, eyes narrowing, 'Fancy the man, do you, my girl?' To which there had been no conceivable answer, and she had blushed wildly, much to her father's glee. By the time she had got round to babbling something nonsensical about spiritual bonding being the most important thing in a relationship, he had been beside himself with laughter.

With one swift, angry movement, she ran her fingers through her braid, untangling it back into its normal, copper tumble. Then she did one final check in the mirror, grabbed her bag and popped in to see her father, who seemed inclined to carry on his in-depth analysis of a man he had never met in his life.

'You're making a big mistake!' he carolled out to her departing back. She was smiling as she left the house because every word that left her father's mouth showed her how much he cared, and that filled her up like nothing else could.

He had made all sorts of crazy assumptions about her and Andreas. She could see that he might have put two and two together when they had been working, sharing jokes, maybe even giving off that intangible intimacy that lovers could give off without even being aware of it. She had thought they had been very discreet at the time, but James had laser vision when it came to reading people. Well, all the more reason to prove to him once and for all that wherever his suspicions lay, they would have to continue to lie there. If not Tom, then she would bring some other chap home at some point. Someone nice. Someone James would quite probably dismiss with a wave of his hand and a disgruntled insult. Someone the complete opposite of Andreas, because she wanted to hang on to her sanity.

Tom was waiting for her in the restaurant, and Elizabeth plastered a warm smile on her face, because he really did look like the kind of guy she should be showing a keen interest in. Tallish, blondish, with brown, kind eyes and an ever so slightly receding hairline. He wasn't the sort of guy who had heads turning in his wake, but then neither was she the sort of girl who had that effect on the opposite sex. It would do her the world of good to get back down to planet Earth, where people didn't have expectations about guys who were way out of their league.

From across the restaurant, Andreas watched with mounting outrage as Elizabeth settled into her chair and leant across the table, smiling at her date. It was filling out nicely, considering it was lunchtime; shouldn't people be at work, for God's sake? Elizabeth's hands were primly on her lap at the moment, but how long before they reached across and invited contact?

His godfather had obviously not been lying when he had hot-footed it to the phone to tell him that she was seeing someone and it might be serious.

'And what, exactly, am I supposed to do with that information?' Andreas had duly queried.

'Do what you like with it,' James had said petulantly. 'But I think I ought to tell you that I've done a few background checks and the guy's not kosher. Put it this way—I wouldn't want my daughter to become a target for gold-diggers and money grabbers.'

'The man's a gold-digger?'

'Very well might be!'

'You know that for a fact?'

'Nothing in life is certain, but tongues wag, lad…if you know what I mean. Call me crazy, but I'd like you to check him out. Wouldn't want the lass to come to any harm. I'm an old man, son…don't think the ticker could take it. You want to put my mind at rest, don't you? Here's the name of the restaurant…just have a look. Must go now, Andreas, this whole thing has quite put me out of sorts. Think I need a lie down…'

Andreas knew his godfather like the back of his hand and he had been deeply suspicious of that wheedling, honeyed tone of voice, but he had shelved all thoughts of pressing for further explanation. Instead, he had leaned back in his leather chair and allowed his mind full rein to run wherever it wanted.

And for the second time in as many weeks he had abandoned the pretence of playing it cool and headed back down to Somerset. He was beginning to know the route like the back of his hand, whether by car, train or helicopter. This time, however, he would not be arriving with any illusions. He was obeying the demands of his gut instincts, and his godfather's insubstantial, waffling concerns about gold-diggers and money grabbers had provided him with a thinly veiled excuse to do precisely what he wanted to do.

Andreas had no intention of walking away from the fortuitous opportunity that had presented itself to him. He was nobody's fool, and indeed matters had resolved themselves in a very handy manner as far as he was concerned.

All meetings for the day had been cancelled within minutes.

He stood up now from where he had asked to be seated, at the back of the room, half-hidden by a pot plant that seemed to be aspiring for a part in *Jack and The Beanstalk.* He tossed his serviette on the table along with more than sufficient money to cover the cost of the salad he had half-eaten, and the two glasses of wine he had drunk with considerably more enthusiasm.

He noticed that no wine had been brought to *their* table. Mineral water all round. Normally, that would have been enough for him to make some healthy and instant character-assassination—because what kind of man took a woman out to lunch and indulged her with water? But a sudden, disconcerting feeling of uncertainty swept through his body like a virus.

He just wished that he could see Elizabeth's face. Even when she was in the middle of pushing him away, he could always tell exactly what was going through her mind by her eyes. However, she was seated with her back to him, and it was only when he drew up at the table that her date eventually broke off his conversation to look up at him with a puzzled frown.

'Yes? Can I help you?'

'I think so,' Andreas drawled, circling the table and positioning himself directly in front of Elizabeth, who looked at him with wide, startled eyes, her mouth half-open as though suddenly bereft of the power of speech. Which was precisely how Andreas had wanted to find her, hence the element of surprise. 'I need to talk to your companion, so if you don't mind…?'

Elizabeth recovered quickly, but her heart was thumping because Andreas was the last person in the world she had expected to see. James must have mentioned her lunch date to his godson, maybe implied that she was throwing herself into a mistake. Naturally that would have been manna from heaven for Andreas, who had already proved that he was willing to scare off the competition until he got what he wanted. No marriage, no commitment, but why should that halt him in his tracks? Was he so convinced that he could break down her defences? Had it become some kind of personal challenge to him, because she had been the one to turn him down? He had expected her to take him up on his generous offer to share his bed the second time around—did that mean that, in his eyes, the challenge had been doubled?

Anger spread like a red mist across her eyes and she swallowed hard, fighting it down, because there was no way that she was going to succumb to a screaming fit in public. Not only would it demean her but it would send poor Tom running for cover. Andreas, she imagined, would have a field day if that happened.

'*I* mind.' She rescued Tom from having to stumble his way through to an appropriate response. She gave Tom a reassuring smile. 'Tom, this is Andreas, my father's godson. I kind of *inherited* him along with my dad.'

Andreas didn't rise to the bait. Instead, he pulled out one of the spare chairs at the table and proceeded to sit down. He even called the waiter across and ordered them a bottle of Sauvignon Blanc. 'Teetotal?'

'I never drink at lunchtime,' Tom explained with a look of mild horror. 'Gives me a terrible headache.'

'What do you want, Andreas?' Elizabeth interceded before the conversation could go totally off the rails. She didn't want to, but her eyes were surreptitiously drawn to the impressive figure he cut in a pair of casual, olive-green trousers and hand-made loafers, and a cashmere jumper that screamed elegance. He would have looked amazing in anything, but he looked even more breathtaking than usual. Wasn't this always going to be the problem? The minute she began to try and put her life back on track, he would show up, and suddenly there would be no space in her world for anyone but him. If she wasn't careful, she would be caught in a never-ending stop-start cycle that would be the equivalent of a ball and chain round her ankles. She was suddenly overcome with a feeling of hopelessness.

'In case you haven't noticed, I'm here with a *friend,*' she said with a bit more renewed vigour. 'I can't think of anything you might want to talk to me about, but if there *is* something then it can wait until I'm available. And I'm not available at the moment.'

'Tom.' Andreas poured himself a glass of wine. 'It's Tom, isn't it? I really need to talk to Elizabeth in private.' He shot her a look of brooding intensity, and then said something that halted her outburst in its tracks. 'Please.'

Elizabeth picked up the shadow of hesitation in his voice, and it was almost shocking, because for Andreas hesitancy was an alien concept.

'What is it?' she asked urgently, when Tom had obediently taken his leave. 'What's the matter? Something's wrong, isn't it?' she continued as her mind frantically tried to contrive scenarios. 'It's not like you to…'

'To what?'

'To sound so *uncertain.* As though there's something you need to say but you don't want to say it.' And that could only mean James, because he would always be the enduring link between them. He was the one person alive who could reduce Andreas to uncertainty. Spontaneously, Elizabeth reached out and threaded her fingers through his, barely aware of her gesture. But Andreas, feeling the warmth of her hand against his own, was rocked by the sensation of being a drowning man who'd been flung a life belt. He held her fingers in his hand with the fierceness of someone needing to hold on tightly.

'This isn't where I would have chosen to have this conversation.'

'Just tell me—is it my father? What's wrong?'

'It's not James. Although he *did* send me…' A man needed an excuse to traipse halfway round the country in pursuit of a woman. 'He thought you might be in danger of becoming victim to a gold-digger.'

Relief was almost instantly overcome by the resurgence of her anger. She wriggled to get her hand free and his grip grew ever so slightly more vice-like.

'That's ridiculous.'

'Just what I told him.'

'I thought something was wrong! I don't want you doing this,' she stated baldly.

'Doing what?'

'Trying to ambush my efforts to settle down here. Tom's not a gold-digger.'

'Okay, maybe he's not a gold-digger, but that doesn't mean that he's suitable. Being bored to death wouldn't be a healthy alternative to me.'

'That does it. That really does it!' She snatched her hand away, cursing to herself; no matter how obnoxious he was, he could still bring her common sense crashing down around her like a fragile house of cards. She rummaged in her bag, fishing out some money for the bottle of water she and Tom had shared. They hadn't even had the chance to glance at a menu! Suddenly he assumed the mantle of a lost opportunity. Her eyes flashed as she stood up, pushed her chair back and headed for the door, face burning with embarrassment as she felt the eyes of the other diners pinned with curiosity to the unfolding spectacle.

With one lithe, supple movement, Andreas was on his feet and in her wake, dimly aware that this wasn't going as planned. He had lost his cool and was in danger of losing it further.

'Who was that guy anyway?' he heard himself demand as she left the restaurant at flying speed and took off down the street towards the car park.

'Why?' Elizabeth demanded, not bothering to look at him, because one look always seemed to be enough to make her whirl off-course. 'Have you rushed down here to give me another health warning about other men? Or do you really still think you can get me into bed by scaring off everyone else because you just can't let go of the challenge?'

'What kind of cheapskate takes a woman out and buys her *water?*'

'Maybe,' she answered grittily, spinning round to look at him with her hands on her hips, 'the kind of cheapskate who isn't terrified at the thought of a relationship that might actually go somewhere!' As if there had been any chance of that! Why kid herself? Andreas had infiltrated every pore in her body, and shaking him off was going to be nigh-on impossible. Wild horses, however, wouldn't have dragged that out of her.

Andreas was suddenly struck by the blinding possibility that he might have blown it, that a couple of seconds in the company of a complete wimp might have been his undoing. Complete wimps weren't scared of talking about a future, even if it was only the occasional throwaway remark about a holiday down the line, or plans for the next weekend. Elizabeth didn't want hot sex, no strings attached; maybe it was too late to start compromising on the strings.

'Anyway! What do you care?'

'I'm jealous as hell.'

That brought Elizabeth to a complete standstill. Andreas was most definitely not the jealous type.

'You're *jealous?*'

'So why don't you just go ahead and laugh?' He gazed at her with silent, aggressively masculine defiance. 'I am not ashamed of that,' he added in a challenging voice.

'Why would you be jealous?'

'I don't want to have this conversation with you here.' His car was just within sight, and without waiting for input from her he strode towards it. Elizabeth tripped along behind him, angry that her curiosity was definitely in overdrive.

'Why would you be jealous?' she repeated the second they were sitting in his car, where at least there was the advantage of warmth. Unfortunately, there was also the danger of intimacy in their confined surroundings.

Andreas felt like a man with one foot dangling over the edge of the precipice. Worse, he was a man who no longer had a choice. Even worse than that was the grim reality that he was a man who didn't *want* a choice. 'I don't like thinking of you with other men,' he stated baldly, firing up the engine because it gave him something to do. He eased his car out of its parking space and began driving towards the house.

Elizabeth thumped hard on the warm glow that filled her. She reminded herself that Andreas's jealousy, glorious though it might be, didn't amount to love. Andreas was driven by lust and a perverse need to be the one to do the breaking off. He didn't like the thought of her with other men because he still wanted her. When he stopped wanting her, he would have no difficulty at all in thinking of her with other men because her time would be up. And she just *wouldn't* allow herself to start thinking that any relationship with Andreas was better than no relationship at all. It would be far too easy to be swept along on the misconception that there was no man on the face of the earth comparable to him. Tom might just be a pleasant guy, rather than relationship material, but there were plenty of other fish in the sea. And aiming to catch one that wasn't a Great White would be altogether better for her well being. Maybe not just yet, but in time.

'Where are we going?'

'Not to the house,' Andreas said heavily. 'I don't need James lurking behind corners, spying on our every move.'

'There'll be nothing to *spy* on. I've said everything I have to say.'

'Well, maybe *I* haven't.' He pulled into one of the lay bys and killed his engine, then he angled his long body so that he was facing her.

Elizabeth braced herself for an attack on her senses of which only he was capable. The sudden silence was hot and oppressive, as was his disturbingly steady gaze. She cleared her throat, but her thoroughly scrambled brains were failing to function.

'I'm sorry if I screwed up your lunch date,' he admitted, fishing for information, but she looked at him in silence. 'Did I screw up your lunch date?' Never at a loss for words, Andreas was finding it difficult to collate his thoughts. It didn't make sense that she would meet some guy for ten minutes and see her future in him, but stranger things had been known to happen. Tom might seem like God's gift to womankind if compared to some other guy who had refused to discuss a relationship and had vetoed anything permanent. As *he* had. Andreas broke out in a film of perspiration in the vortex of her continuing silence.

'He'd be no good for you anyway,' Andreas heard himself say.

'You have no idea who would be good for me and who wouldn't!' Elizabeth said fiercely, swinging round to face him. 'How dare you sit there and dictate my life?'

'You belong to me!'

She gave a wild, disbelieving, incredulous screech of laughter. 'I can't believe you just said that! Who do you think you are?'

'I…' Andreas ran his fingers through his hair. He wanted to pull her to him and never let her go. When he thought of her with another man, when he even considered the possibility that he had suffered in comparison to someone else—someone ridiculous who had taken her out and treated her to a glass of water—he saw red. 'I…'

The anger seeped out of Elizabeth, replaced by genuine confusion. She didn't know where he was going or what he was trying to say.

'I haven't been honest with you or with myself,' Andreas muttered thickly. 'Can you blame me? How was I supposed to know that falling in love was like a punch in the gut?'

'Falling in love?' Elizabeth asked, all at sea.

'I've dated a lot of women, and I really thought I knew what I wanted from life.'

'Which was what?' Elizabeth didn't want to say too much just in case she ruined the momentum, which had her pulses racing and her heart pounding, but the thirst for detail was too much to resist.

'Work, first and foremost,' Andreas said in a thoughtful voice, because the fact that work had been pushed into a poor second place was still astounding. 'Like I once told you, I always knew where I came from, and always knew that what I got out of life had to be independent of what James was more than happy to provide. Women were an enjoyable sideline, a bonus that came with the accumulation of power and money.'

'Do you really think that that's all they would have been attracted to?'

Andreas shrugged. 'I never questioned it. Until you came along and threw the whole neat equation into holy disarray.'

Elizabeth smiled. An ability to throw things into disarray now seemed the most wonderful ability in the world.

'I thought that it was just the novelty of having a relationship with a real woman that was the attraction. I thought that it would pass in time, just like all the rest. But then I found myself asking you to move in with me. It was the first time I had ever asked anything like that of any woman.' He laughed and stared broodingly off into the distance, before refocusing on her upturned face. 'When you turned me down…'

'I didn't want to be your mistress, and I was smarting from thinking that Amanda…'

'I'm sure she'll make a fine partner for some guy out there, but for me she was less than nothing. In fact, the minute you came along, I couldn't even remember what the point of any other woman could be. It just took me a long time to work that out.'

Elizabeth's face was glowing. She was finally understanding the depth of emotion it must have taken for him to ask her to move in with him, all the more powerful because he would not have recognised its source at the time.

'When James told me about that party, hell, I didn't want to come but I couldn't help myself. I *had* to come. I realised that I had to do something to get you back. Anything. But I wouldn't rush you. Then Mr Water Boy came along. James hinted that he might have been after your money. I didn't believe him, but I wasn't going to pass up a golden opportunity to come down here…to see you again. Now you know why I'm insane with jealousy.'

Elizabeth smiled a broad, goofy smile. 'I never thought I'd hear you say something like that.'

'Frankly, neither did I. Just goes to show that, when you think you've got life mapped out, you turn your back and the directions have all changed.' He rested his stunning eyes on her shining face and finally succumbed to the temptation to reach out and caress her satin-smooth cheek. 'I don't want to ask you to live with me. I want you to marry me. That's the only way I won't go crazy thinking that I might lose you. But there's one little condition.'

Elizabeth tensed, but he smiled at her, and in that smile she could see love and tenderness and an awkward vulnerability that stole all his natural arrogance.

'You have to tell me that you love me as much I love you.'

'You know I do.' She leaned across the space dividing

them, and as his firm mouth touched hers she gave a little whimper of pure ecstasy.

'Good,' Andreas growled, pulling her towards him. 'I've never made love in a lay by off a country lane in my car, but I think I'm about to change that…'

Against his mouth, Elizabeth giggled, and gasped as his hand made its way under her clothes to find her burning skin underneath. 'What,' she asked breathlessly, 'do you think James is going to make of this?'

'I think,' Andreas replied, while still capable of coherent speech, 'that the wily old fox will think that *his* best-laid plans have gone exactly as he hoped.'